Shadows & Moonshine

SHADOWS &

DAVID R. GODINE

PUBLISHER · BOSTON

MOONSHINE

stories by JOAN AIKEN

illustrations by Pamela Johnson

First published in 2001 by
DAVID R. GODINE · *Publisher*
Post Office Box 450
Jaffrey, New Hampshire 03452
www.godine.com

LIBRARY OF CONGRESS CATALOGING-IN-PUBLICATION DATA
Aiken, Joan, 1924–
Shadows and moonshine : stories / by Joan Aiken ;
[illustrated by Pamela Johnson].
p. cm.
Contents: Boy with a wolf's foot — Gift pig —
Rain Child — Night the stars were gone —
Moonshine in the mustard pot — Cat's cradle —
Small pinch of weather — Lilac in the lake —
Rocking Donkey — King who stood all night —
Cooks and prophecies — John Sculpin and
the witches — Wolves and the mermaids.
ISBN 1–56792–167–1 (hardcover : alk. paper)
1. Children's stories, English. [1. Short stories.]
I. Johnson, Pamela, ill. II. Title.
PZ7.A2695 Sj 2001 2004
[fic]—dc21 2001023830

FIRST SOFTCOVER PRINTING, 2008
Printed in the United States of America

Contents

Introduction

———•———

Rereading these stories, written over a span of nearly fifty years, aroused in me a whole flood of memories, as well as some thoughts about the writing of short stories.

A short story, I believe, should have at least two different narrative strands in it. Long ago I worked as editorial assistant on a short-story magazine in England, and one of my tasks was to interview the writers whose works we printed, and ask them about their methods of writing. H. E. Bates, who wrote beautiful stories about English country characters, told me that for him a story always needed two different ideas to get it off the ground, to make it begin working and fermenting in his mind. I thought about this and realized that the story writing process was exactly the same for me. Out of nowhere you are suddenly given the basic thread — a person is lent a book by someone who then dies quite unexpectedly — how then can the person return the book, discuss its importance, what can he do with that book now?

I have walked about, sometimes for months, with part of

a story like this dangling in my brain, waiting for the fertilizing agent to arrive and mix tile ingredients together, start them growing and shaping into a live structure. Sometimes it never happens. Sometimes it happens the next day. Sometimes years go by.

A very important element in a story is the setting — the scene where it takes place. Eleven of the stories in this collection have their settings and surroundings so firmly in my mind that I can call them back whenever I want to. *A Small Pinch of Weather* is set in the town of Lewes, in Sussex, where I once lived next door to a guest-house where a Bishop regularly came to stay. *The Boy with a Wolf's Foot* was written when I travelled back and forth to London every day along a railway line whose stations all seemed to begin with *W*. *The Rain Child* came when I had a job picking apples in a huge series of orchards. *The Night the Stars Were Gone* was triggered by a visit to the Museum of Modern Art in New York, which has a mysterious little garden surrounded by high walls. *Moonshine in the Mustard Pot* is a mixture of Paris and the beautiful city of York in England. My daughter lived for a time in both these cities and I visited her there, and the grandmother in the story is a mix of my daughter and myself. *Lilac in the Lake* is from a lovely village in Yorkshire where I used to spend holidays with my brothers. *A Harp of Fishbones* is purely invention, but I know that mountainside, that ruined city as well as if I had lived there all my life. *Cat's Cradle* takes place in the seaside town of Whitstable, where my husband and I once kept a sailboat. The stories that have the strongest settings are my favorites; I like to revisit them from time to time, and that is like going back to stay in a house, or piece of country, that one has known since childhood; it is a happy, refreshing thing to do. Reading is and always will be one of my greatest pleasures. And I love to reread books that have been favorites for years: *Pride and Prejudice*, *Jane Eyre*, *The Secret Garden*, *The Princess and the Goblin*. Reading is like stepping into somebody else's mind, a holiday from oneself. I don't — very much — re-read my own full-length novels, unless I am obliged to for some professional reason, checking a point of plot for a sequel or reading a proof. Novels are written and planned much more slowly and methodically than short stories. The planning can go on for months.

But stories just arrive — like tornadoes — one minute they are on top of you, next minute, unless you grab them, they are gone. And I like to re-visit some of my short stories particularly. Stories are fun to write. They are, or should be, like a sleigh-ride — you get on course, and then some terrific power, like the power of gravity, takes command and whizzes you off to an unknown destination. When I was working on *Argosy*, the short-story magazine, forty years ago, I would grab at the skirts of two stories, as I rode homewards on the train from London to Sussex, and then write them both as soon as I got home.

I couldn't do that now, I would not have the needful energy — writing takes a lot of that. I can remember, almost fifty years ago, when I was running a guest house in Cornwall, peeling potatoes in the kitchen, talking to a boy called Nicky, one of the guests, planning tomorrow's meals with half my mind, and writing a story called *Cricket* with the other half of my mind. I couldn't do that now, either.

But still, every now and then, the voice of a short story

whispers in my ear. (Each story has its own particular voice. When I think of people I know, who have died, it is not their faces I remember, but their voices, and the way they said things; faces alter, but voices have their own resonance, their own key, forever. It is the same with stories). So — every now and then the voice of a story whispers in my ear, and if I am lucky, and can catch hold of the second, necessary, fertilizing ingredient — and don't have too many other distracting commitments battling for my attention — then, then I can sit down and write, "Once there was a boy called Fred whose uncle lent him a book . . ." and, so long as the phone doesn't ring just then, I am off and away.

— *Joan Aiken*

Shadows & Moonshine

The Gift Pig

Once upon a time there was a king whose queen, having just presented him with a baby princess, unfortunately died. The king was very upset and grieved, but he had to go on with the arrangements for the christening just the same, as court etiquette was strict on this point. What with his grief and distraction, however, and the yells of the royal baby, who was extremely lively and loud-voiced, the invitations to the christening were sent out very carelessly, and by mistake the list included two elderly fairies who were known to loathe the very sight of one another, though when seen alone they were pleasant enough.

The day of the christening arrived, and at first all went well. The baby princess was christened Henrietta and behaved properly, crying a little but not too much. Then the guests strolled back to the palace for the reception, and the king noticed with horror that the two elderly fairies were walking side by side. They seemed to be nodding and smiling in the most friendly way, but when the king edged nearer to them he heard one say: "Really, my dear Bella, do you think it wise for you to come out in this chilly weather? You walk with such a limp! I wish you had asked me to wheel you in your bath chair."

"How sweet of you, my dearest Gorgonzola, but could you manage it? Didn't you celebrate your hundredth birthday last week? And in any case, I don't have a bath chair."

"No? You surprise me. And what surprises me still more is to see you in the palace of this commonplace king — can it be that you are now so poor you have to go anywhere on the chance of a free meal?"

"Hardly that, my dear Gorgonzola. I came out of politeness. I confess I didn't expect to see you here. I understood the king only invited intelligent and progressive people."

The poor king made haste to cut the cake and circulate the sherry in the hope of sweetening these acid ladies.

Presently the guests, fairy and otherwise, began to bring forward their gifts. The baby, pink and good in her cradle, was given silver and coral rattles, bonnets and booties by the basketful, mountains of matinee jackets and mittens, stacks of embroidered smocks and knitted socks. Besides this, she was endowed with good health, a friendly disposition, a cheerful nature, intelligence and a logical mind.

Then the Fairy Bella stepped forward and, smiling sweetly at the king, said, "You will forgive me if my gift is not quite so pleasant as some of the preceding ones, but meeting such low company in your palace has made me forget myself a little. Let the princess rue the day that someone gives her a pig, for when that happens she will turn into one herself."

"Moreover," said the Fairy Gorgonzola, "she will marry someone with only one leg."

"Wait a minute, you insolent person. I hadn't finished. The princess will lose her inheritance — "

"I was going to say there will be a revolution — "

"Will you please be quiet. There will not be a revolution — at least the princess herself will be lost long before that occurs and she will be poor and unknown and have to work for her living."

"And she will marry someone who has spent all his life in the open."

"Oh for goodness' sake! Didn't I just say she would marry someone with only one leg."

"The two things aren't mutually exclusive."

"You don't very often find agricultural workers with only one leg."

"Ladies, ladies," said the king miserably, but not daring to be too abrupt with them, "you have done enough harm to my poor child. Will you please continue your quarrel somewhere else?"

The feuding fairies left, and the king hung with tears in his eyes over the beautiful pink baby, wondering what, if anything, he could do to avert the various bits of evil fortune that were coming to her. The only thing that seemed to lie within his power was to keep a strict watch over her presents in order to make sure that she was never given a pig.

When Henrietta was five years old her cousin Lord Edwin Fitzlion came to stay with her. He was a spoiled, wild, boy of about the same age; he was the seventh son of a seventh son, but his brothers were all much older and had gone off into the world, his father was a big game hunter and never at home, while his mother had grown tired of looking after the boys and had gone off on a three year cruise. Lord Edwin had been left in the care of the butler.

He was very beautiful, with dark velvety eyes and black

hair, much better looking than his fat pink cousin; he was inclined to tease her.

One day he overheard two footmen discussing the fairies' pronouncements about her, and he became consumed with curiosity as to whether she would really turn into a pig if she were given one. He longed to give her a pig and find out. There were difficulties about bringing pigs into the palace, but at last he managed to buy one from a heavily bribed farmer and smuggled it in, wrapped up in his jacket. He let it loose in the nursery and then rushed in search of Henrietta.

"Henry come quick, I've brought a present for you."

"Oh, where?"

"In the nursery! Hurry up!"

With rare politeness he stood aside to let her go first and heard her squeak of joy as she ran through the door: "Oh, it's a dear little pi — "

Then there was silence, except for squeaks, and when he went in he found two dear little pigs, absolutely identical, rubbing noses in the most friendly way.

Lord Edwin was sent home in disgrace. His parents were still away (in fact they never came home) and he ran wild and spent all his time in the woods, riding his eldest brother's horse Bayard and flying his next brother's falcon Ger. One day when he was in the forest he saw a large hare on the bank of a pool. Quickly he unhooded the falcon, when the hare suddenly spoke: "Don't do it! You'll be sorry if you do."

"Oh who cares for you," said Edwin rudely, and he loosed Ger. But the falcon, instead of towering up and then dropping on the hare, flew slantwise and then turned and made for home. Edwin's eyes followed the bird in annoyance and disappointment. When he looked back he saw that the hare had become a little old woman.

"You're a spoiled and disobedient boy," she said. "I know all about you, and what you did to your cousin. You can stay where you are, learning better manners, until a home Secretary comes to rescue you."

No one had been fond of Edwin, so no one missed him or asked where he was.

The king was heartbroken when he learned what had happened to his daughter. Many tests were carried out on the two little pigs to try and discover which was the princess. They were put into little beds with peas under the mattresses, but both rummaged out the peas and ate them during the night. Two dishes, one of pearls, one of potato peelings, were placed in front of them, in the hope that the princess would prefer the pearls, but they both dived unhesitatingly for the potato peelings. The first pig breeders in the land were brought to gaze at them, but with no result; they were two big handsome little pigs, and that was all that could be said about them.

"Well," said the king finally, "one of them is my daughter, and she must receive the education due to a princess. Someday she will be restored to her proper shape (we know this because she is going to marry a one legged man, poor dear).

"The fairy didn't actually say a man with one leg," someone pointed out.

"Well, what else could it be — you've never seen a pig with one leg. Anyway she must have a proper education. It would be terrible if she were restored to human form and only had the knowledge of a child of five."

So the two little pigs sat seriously and attentively side by side on two little chairs and were taught and lectured by a series of tutors and erudite schoolmistresses. No one could tell if any of the teaching sank in, for they merely sat and gazed. If they were asked questions, they grunted.

One day when the pigs were about fifteen the king came into the schoolroom.

"Hullo, my dears," he said, "how are you today?" He patted his daughter and her friend and sat down wearily in an armchair, to watch while they had their lunch. Affairs of state were becoming very tiring to him.

A footman brought in two little blue bowls of pig mash on a silver tray. The pigs' eyes gleamed, and they let out piercing squeals and began to rush about frantically bumping into tables and chairs and each other. Their governess firmly collared them one at a time, tied a frilly bib around each neck, and strapped them into two high chairs. Their bowls were put in front of them, and instantly there was such a guzzling and a slurping and greedy slobbering that no one could hear a word for five minutes until the bowls were empty. Then the little pigs looked up again, brimming with satisfaction, their faces encircled by rings of mash.

The footman wiped their faces clean with a clean cloth-of-gold facecloth. Then they were let out into the garden to play and could be seen whisking around and around the trees and chasing each other up and down the paths.

The king sighed.

"It's no use," he said. "One must face facts. My daughter Henrietta is not an ordinary princess. And her friend Hermione — whichever of them is which — is a very ordinary little pig. I am afraid that no prince, even a one-legged one, would ask for Henrietta's hand in marriage after seeing her eat her lunch. We must send them to a finishing school. They've had plenty of intellectual education — at least I suppose they have — it's time they acquired a bit of polish."

So the two pigs were packed off (in hampers) to *Miss Dorothea ffoulkes' Select Finishing School for the Daughters of the Monarchy and Aristocracy.*

At first all went well. The king received monthly reports which informed him that his daughter (and her friend) had learned to walk downstairs with books on their heads, to enter and leave rooms gracefully, get in and out of motors with dignity and elegance, play the piano and the harp, waltz, embroider, and ride sidesaddle.

"Well I always heard that Miss ffoulkes was a marvel," said the king, shaking his head in astonishment, "but I never thought anyone could teach a pig to ride sidesaddle. I can't wait to see them."

He had to wait though. Miss ffoulkes strictly forbade the parents of her pupils to come and visit them while they are being put through their course of training. The reason for this was that she had to treat the girls with such frightful severity in order to drill the necessary elegance and deportment in to them that if they had the chance they would have implored their parents to take them away. Letters home were always dictated by Miss ffoulkes herself, so there was no opportunity of complaining by post, and at the end of the course the debutantes were so grateful for their beautiful poise that all was forgotten and forgiven.

Miss ffoulkes nearly met her Waterloo in Henrietta and Hermione.

She managed to teach them tennis and bridge, but she could not teach them flower arrangement. The two pigs had no taste for it — they always ate the flowers.

One day they had been spanked and sent out into the garden in disgrace for eating a large bundle of roses and sweet peas instead of building them into a table center. Sore, bewildered and miserable, they wandered down the dreary gravel paths, and then simultaneously the notion came to them — why not run away? They wriggled through the hedge at the bottom of the garden and disappeared.

Instead of a final report on deportment the king had a note from Miss ffoulkes saying: "I regret to announce that your daughter and her friend have committed the unpardonable social blunder of running away from my establishment. The police have been informed, and will no doubt recover them for you in due course. Since this behavior shows chat that my tuition has been thrown away on them your fees are returned herewith. (Check for £10,000 encl.) Your obdt. srvt., Dorothea ffoulkes."

In spite of all efforts the police failed to trace the two little pigs. Advertisements in newspapers and on radio and television, pictures outside police stations, offers of rewards all brought no replies. The king was in terror, imagining his daughter and her friend innocently running into a bacon factory. He gave up all attempt at governing and spent his time going from farm to farm gazing mournfully at all the pigs in hope of recognizing Henrietta and her friend.

The two pigs had not gone very far — in fact, no farther than the garden of the house next door to Miss ffoulkes. They were rooting peacefully (but elegantly because their training had stuck) near the front gate when they saw a young man in a white coat coming down the path from the house escorting a pretty young lady. "And don't forget," she was saying earnestly, "all the last experimental results are in the stack under the five-gram weight, and the milk for the tea is in the test tube at the left-hand end of the right-hand rack, and the baby amoeba wants feeding again at five. Now I must fly or my fiancé will be worrying."

"Good-bye, Miss Sparks," said the young man crossly, and he slammed the gate behind her. "Why in the name of goodness do all my assistants have to get married. Pigs, would you like a job as research assistants?

The pigs liked his face, which was a friendly one, and followed him into his house, where he proceeded to instruct them in the research work he was doing.

"I shall have to teach you to talk though," he told them. "I can't put up with assistants who grunt all the time."

He left his other work and devoted himself to teaching them. At the end of a week he had succeeded, for he was a scientist and a philosopher, besides being a very brilliant man. Nobody had ever considered teaching pigs to talk before.

When they could speak, the professor asked their names.

"One of us is Henrietta and one is Hermione, but we are not sure which," they told him.

"In that case I shall call you Miss X and Miss Y. Miss X, you will look after making the tea, feeding the amoeba and filing the microscope slides. Miss Y you will turn away all visitors, polish the microscope, and make notes of my experiments."

The two pigs now found their education most useful. They could carry piles of books on their heads, curtsy to callers as they showed them to the door, write notes in a neat little round hand, and play the piano to soothe the professor if the experiments were not going well. They were all very happy together, and the professor often said that he had never before had such useful and talented assistants.

One day, after several years had passed by, the professor raised his eye from the microscope, rubbed his forehead, looked at Miss Y industriously taking notes and Miss X busily putting away all her slides, and said, "Pigs, it occurs to me to wonder if you are really human beings turned into your present useful, if unornamental form?"

"One of us is," replied Miss X tucking her pencil behind her ear, "but we don't know which."

"It would be easy enough to change you back," the professor remarked. "I wonder I never thought of it before. I'll just switch on the cosmic ray and rearrange your molecules."

"Which of us?"

"You can both try, and I expect nothing will happen to one of you."

"Shall we like that?" said the pigs to each other. "We're used to being together."

"Oh, come on," exclaimed the professor impatiently, "if one of you is human it's her plain duty to change back, and the other one shouldn't stand in her way."

Thus admonished the pigs walked in front of the ray and both immediately turned into young ladies with pink faces, turned-up noses, fair hair, and intelligent blue eyes.

"Dear me," remarked the professor, "that ray must be more powerful than I had thought. We seem to be back where we were."

As the young ladies still did not know which of them was which, they continued to be called Miss X and Miss Y, and as they were very happy in their work, they continued to help the professor.

One day Miss Y saw a large number of callers coming to the front door, and though she did her best to turn them back they poured in and overflowed into the laboratory.

"Professor," said the spokesman, "we are the leaders of the revolution, and we have come to ask you to be first president of our new republic, as you are undoubtedly the wisest man in the country."

"Tut, tut," said the professor frowning, "why have you revolted, and what have you done with the king?"

"Oh, we revolted because it was the fashionable thing to do — all the other countries have done it already — and the king has retired already and taken to farming. But now please step into the carriage which is waiting outside, and we will take you to the new president's residence."

"If I accept," said the Professor, "I must have unlimited time to pursue my own research."

"Yes, yes, you will have to do very little governing — just keep an eye on things and see that justice and reason prevail. You can appoint anyone you like to whatever government positions you wish.

"In that case I shall appoint two assistants, Miss X and Miss Y, to be in charge of home and foreign affairs respectively. No one could be more efficient."

The professor and Miss X and Miss Y were driven to the new president's residence which turned out to be none other than the ancestral home of the Fitzlion family, where Edwin had once run wild in the woods. After drafting some sensible acts, Miss X, the secretary of state for home affairs, took a stroll in the woods, for when she was a pig she had been very fond of acorns and she still took an absent-minded pleasure in putting them in her pockets.

She had not gone far when she stood still and listened attentively. It seemed to her that one of the trees was sighing and sobbing.

"Are you in distress?" she said to the tree kindly. "Can I help you?"

"Oh, if only you could!" the tree lamented. "Many years ago I was turned into a tree as a punishment for my bad behavior, and I am so terribly bored in these woods! But only a home secretary can help me."

"I am a home secretary."

"You! You are much too beautiful and charming to be a home secretary," said the tree in astonishment. Miss X beamed. No one had spoken to her like this before.

The new president was looking through his microscope that evening when Miss X came to see him, starry-eyed.

"I've fallen in love," she announced.

The professor sighed. "It was bound to happen sooner or later. With whom?"

"With an enchanted tree in the woods. I wish you would turn your cosmic ray on him and change him back into a human being."

"By and by," grumbled the professor, "when we've got this present series of experiments finished." He wanted to make sure of his assistant for as long as possible.

However, Miss X and the tree were so much in love that they got the archbishop to come and marry them, and when the professor saw that they were in earnest he trundled his cosmic ray projector out into the forest and turned it on the tree, which at once became a handsome young man, while a raven who had been sitting on one of the branches turned into an elderly fairy.

"Tampering with the laws of nature, I call it," she said looking sourly at the projector. "Anyway, at least Lord Edwin's learned some manners now, though that princess is still as plain a piece as I ever saw."

Muttering crossly to herself the fairy Gorgonzola flapped

away, and now, of course, Henrietta knew who she was, and also realized that she had fulfilled the prophecies by marrying a man with one leg who had lived all his life in the open.

Arm in arm the happy couple went to visit the old king, who was perfectly contented on his farm and thankful to have left off governing. He was delighted to see his daughter again.

"I am sure that you young people can manage very well without me, and Henrietta will make just as good a home secretary as she would a queen. As for me, I have got into the habit of looking at pigs, and I much prefer to go on doing so." And he scratched the back of a large black.

So Lord Edwin became prime minister (having learned tact and diplomatic manners during his long spell as a tree). Miss Y, who was now known to be Hermione, married the professor, and they all lived happily ever after.

The Rocking Donkey

———— ◆ ————

There was once a little girl called Esmeralda who lived with her wicked stepmother. Her father was dead. The stepmother, who was called Mrs Mitching, was very rich, and lived in a large but hideous house in a suburb with a dusty, laurelly garden, an area, and a lot of ornamental iron fencing.

Mrs Mitching was fond of opening things, and getting things up. The things she opened were mostly hospitals or public libraries, or new bypasses, or civic centers, and the things she got up were sales of work, and bazaars, and flag days. She was in fact a public figure, and was very little at home. When she was, she spent her time receiving callers in her fringy, ornamented drawing room.

"How is your little girl?" they would sometimes ask. "Is she still at home, or has she gone to boarding school?"

"Oh, she's at home," Mrs Mitching would reply, "but she has her own playroom, you know, so that we needn't disturb one another. I don't believe in grownups bothering children all the time, do you?"

Mrs Mitching could not afford school for Esmeralda, as she needed all her wealth for opening and getting up. She always took Esmeralda along to the openings, in a white muslin dress, painfully starched at the neck and wrists, because people liked to see a child on the platform.

But for the rest of the time Esmeralda had to manage in her old brown dress, much too short now, and a torn pair of gym shoes. She had her meals in the kitchen, and they were horrible — bread and margarine, boiled fish, and prunes.

But the most melancholy part of Esmeralda's life was that she had nothing to do. The playroom which Mrs Mitching spoke of was a large dark basement room, shadowed by the laurels which overhung the area. There was nothing in it at all, not even a chair. No one ever came into it, and it would have been thick with dust had not Esmeralda, who was a tidy creature, once a week borrowed a broom from the housemaid's cupboard and swept it. She had no toys. Once Mr Snye, the man who came to cut the laurels, had given her a length of garden twine, and she used this as a skipping rope, to keep herself warm. She became a very good skipper, and could polka, double-through, swing the rope, and other fancy variations, while if she felt inclined to do plain skipping she could go on almost all day without a fault.

There were no books to read in the house, and she was not encouraged to go into Mrs Mitching's rooms or outside because of her shabby clothes, though she sometimes took a stroll at dusk.

One day Mrs Mitching was to open a jumble sale. She was being driven to it by the mayor in his Rolls-Royce, so she told Hooper, the housemaid, to bring Esmeralda by bus, dressed in her white muslin, and meet her at the hall. Then she went off to keep an appointment.

"Drat," said Hooper. "Now what am I to do? Your muslin's still at the laundry from last week."

"I'll have to go as I am," said Esmeralda, who quite liked openings. At least they made a change from wandering about in the basement.

"I don't know what Madam'll say," said Hooper doubtfully, "but I should catch it if I didn't take you, sure enough." So they went as they were, Esmeralda in her old brown dress and shoes.

When Mrs Mitching saw them she gave a cry of dismay, "I can't let you be seen like that! You must go home at once," and she hurriedly left them, before anyone should connect her with the shabby child.

Hooper had set her heart on a violet satin pincushion she had noticed on one of the stalls, so she pushed Esmeralda into a corner, and said, "You wait there, I shan't be a moment. It won't matter, no one will know who you are."

Esmeralda stood looking quietly about her. An elderly gentleman, Lord Mauling, making his way to the platform, noticed what seemed to him a forlorn-looking little creature, and stopping by her he took a coin from his pocket and said, "Here, my dear. Buy yourself a pretty toy."

Esmeralda gave him a startled look as he went on his way, and then stared at the coin she held in her hand. It was a shilling. She had never had any money before and was quite puzzled to know what she should buy with it. Almost without realizing what she was doing she began to wander along the stalls, looking at the different things offered for sale. There were books, clothes, bottles of scent, flowers — all the things she saw seemed beautiful, but she could not imagine buying any of them. Then she came to the toy counter. Toys! She had never had one. The only time she ever touched a toy was sometimes when Mrs Mitching opened a children's ward at a hospital, and Esmeralda would present a ceremonial teddy bear to a little patient. She gazed at dolls, puzzles, engines, without noticing that most of them were shabby and second-hand. Then at the end of the counter she saw what she wanted; there was no hesitation in her mind, she knew at once.

It was a rocking donkey — gray, battered, weather-beaten, with draggling ears and tangled tail. On the side of his rockers his name was painted "Prince." It hardly seemed the name for someone so ancient and worn. And the price ticket pinned to his tail said one shilling.

"I'd like the donkey, please," said Esmeralda timidly to the lady at the stall, holding out her coin. The lady glanced from the coin to the ticket and said, "good gracious. Can this really be going for only a shilling? Surely they mean ten? Mr Prothero," she called to a gentleman farther down the room, but he was busy and did not hear.

"Oh well," she said to Esmeralda. "You take it. You won't often get a bargain like that, I can tell you." She took the coin, and lifted the donkey down onto the floor.

"How will you get him home?" she asked.

"I don't know," said Esmeralda. She was lucky though. As she stood hesitating with her hand on Prince's bridle, someone familiar stopped beside her. It was Mr Snye, the man who cut the hedges.

"You bought that donkey?" he said. "Well I'm blest. That'll be a bit of fun for you, I reckon. Like me to take it home for you in the van? I've got it outside — been bringing some flowers along for the platform."

"Oh thank you," Esmeralda said. So he shouldered

Prince, nodded to her and said, "I'll be home before you are, like as not. I'll just leave him in the shrubbery for you."

Esmeralda went to find Hooper, who had bought her pincushion, and they caught their bus home.

As soon as dusk fell, and no one was about, she slipped up the back steps and half dragged, half carried Prince from his hiding place down through the basement passage to her playroom. She put him in the middle of the floor, and sat down beside him.

It was a strange moment. For as long as she could remember she had had no company at all, nothing to play with, and now here, all of a sudden, was a friend. She felt sure of that. She put an arm over his cold smooth neck, and he rocked down and gently touched the top of her head with his nose.

"Prince," she said quietly, and almost wondered if he would reply, but he was silent. She combed out his tangled mane and tail, and sat with him until the room was quite dark and it was time to put herself to bed.

As she went to her tiny room upstairs it occurred to her that he might be cold, alone in that dark basement. She took one of the two blankets off her bed, slipped down again in her nightdress, and tucked it over him. Back in bed she tried to settle but could not; it was a chilly night and one blanket was not enough to keep her warm. Also, she could not help wondering if Prince felt lonely and perhaps homesick for wherever he had come from? So presently she was tiptoeing back to the playroom with the other blanket. She made a sort of nest for the two of them, and slept all night on the floor, curled up between his front rockers so that if she wanted company, all she had to do was reach up and pull on a rein, to bring down his cold friendly nose against her cheek.

She was never lonely again. She never rode on Prince — she felt that would be almost an impertinence with someone who was so much a friend, and who moreover looked so weary and battered. But she would set him off rocking while she skipped, so that they seemed to be keeping each other company, and she talked to him all the time, while he nodded intelligently in reply. And every night she crept down with her two blankets and slept curled up between his feet.

One day Mrs Mitching decided to give a whist drive in her house for the wives of chimney sweeps, and it occurred to her that the basement playroom would be just the right size for the purpose. She went along to inspect it, and found Esmeralda having her weekly cleanout with brush and dustpan.

"That's right, that's right," she said absently, glancing about. "But what is this? A rocking horse?" Esmeralda stood mute.

"Do you not think you are a little old for such toys? Yes, yes, I think it had better be given away to some poor child. It is the duty of children who live in rich houses, such as you, Esmeralda, to give away your old toys to the little slum children who have nothing. It can be taken away when the van for the Bombed Families calls here tomorrow morning. But you must certainly clean it up a little first. You should be quite ashamed to pass on such a shabby old toy without doing your best to improve its appearance. After all, you know, it may gladden some poor little life in Stepney or Bethnal Green. So give it a good scrub this evening. Now what was I doing? Ah, yes, seventeen feet by sixteen, ten tables — let me see. . . ."

Esmeralda passed the rest of the day in a sort of numbness. After tea she took some sugar soap and a scrubbing brush from the housemaid's cupboard and started to scrub Prince.

"Well," she thought, "perhaps I didn't deserve to be so happy. I never thought of scrubbing him. Perhaps someone else will take better care of him. But oh, what shall I do, what shall I do?"

She scrubbed and scrubbed, and as the shabby gray peeled away, a silvery gleam began to show along Prince's back and sides, and his mane and tail shone like floss. By the time she had finished, it was quite dark, and a long ray of moonlight, striking across the floor, caught his head and for a moment dazzled her eyes.

For the last time she went up, fetched her blankets, and settled herself beside him. Just before she fell asleep it seemed to her that his nose came down and lightly touched her wet cheek.

Next day Esmeralda hid herself. She did not want to see Prince taken away. Mrs Mitching superintended his removal.

"Good gracious," she said, when she saw him shining in the sun. "That is far too valuable to be taken to Stepney. I shall give it to the museum." So the Bombed Families van dropped Prince off at the museum before going on to Stepney.

All day Esmeralda avoided the basement playroom. She felt that she could not bear to look at the empty patch in the middle of the floor.

In the evening Hooper felt sorry for her, she seemed so restless and moping, and took her out for a stroll. They went to the museum, where Hooper liked to look at the models of fashions through the ages. While she was studying crinolines and bustles Esmeralda wandered off, and soon, around a corner, she came on Prince, railed off from the public with a red cord, and a notice beside him which read, "Donated by the Hon. Mrs Mitching, November 19 — "

Esmeralda stretched out her hand, but she could not quite touch him over the cord.

"Now, miss," said an attendant. "No touching the exhibits, please." So she looked and looked at him until Hooper said it was time to go home.

Every day after that she went to the museum and looked at Prince, and Hooper said to Cook, "That child doesn't look well." Mrs Mitching was away from home a good deal, organizing the grand opening of a new welfare center and clinic, so she did not notice Esmeralda's paleness, or her constant visits to the museum.

One night something woke Esmeralda. It was a long finger of moonlight which lay lightly across her closed eyes. She got up quietly and put on her old brown dress and thin shoes. It was easy to steal out of that large house without anyone hearing, and once outside she slipped along the empty streets like a shadow. When she reached the museum she went at once, as if someone had called her, to a little door at one side. Someone had left it unlocked, and she opened it softly and went into the thick dark.

The museum was a familiar place by now, and she went confidently forward along a passage, and presently came out into the main hall. It did not take her long to find Prince, for there he was, shining like silver in the moonlight. She walked forward, stepped over the rope, and put her hand on his neck.

"Esmeralda," he said. His voice was like a faint, silvery wind.

"You never spoke to me before."

"How could I? I was choked with gray paint."

"Oh," she cried, "I'm so terribly lonely without you. What shall I do?"

"You never rode on me," he said.

"I didn't like to. You were so old and tired, it would have seemed like taking a liberty."

"Ride on me now."

Timidly she put her foot into the stirrup and swung herself onto his back.

"Settle yourself in the saddle and hold tight. Are you all right?"

"Yes," she said.

Like a feather in the wind they went rocking up the ray of moonlight and passed through the high window as if it had been a mist. Neither of them was ever seen again.

Cooks and Prophecies

This time we'll have an entirely private christening," said the king to the queen. "You remember what a time we had with fairies when Florizel was christened — all of them canceling out each other's gifts till in the end the poor boy had nothing at all."

"Very well, dear," said the queen sadly. But she loved parties, and in spite of the warning she could not resist inviting just one or two old friends. She did not invite the wicked fairy Gorgonzola.

On the day after the christening she received by post a little note written in red ink on black paper. "Dear Queen," it read, "I was charmed to read about your christening party in yesterday's evening papers. I quite understand that you would not wish to be bothered with an old fogey like myself, so I shall not trouble you by calling, but have sent my christening present to the princess by registered post. Yours affectionately, Gorgonzola."

Filled with alarm the queen rushed off to the nursery in

order to prevent, if possible, the wicked fairy's parcel from being opened. Too late! The head nurse had already undone the paper and string, and was just then opening a dear little gold casket before the baby's wondering eyes.

The horror-stricken queen saw a small cloud of black smoke rise from the casket and envelop the princess's head. When it cleared away she had become the ugliest baby born in that kingdom for a hundred years.

At that moment, however, a passing bird dropped a prophecy down the palace chimney. This said:

Seek not Griselda's fortune in her looks
Remember better things are found in books.

This comforted the king, who would otherwise have been inclined to say "I told you so," and he therefore occupied himself by laying out a grand scheme for Griselda's education, for he presumed that this was what the rhyme meant. Though, as the piece of paper on which it was written was very sooty, and the writing on it bad, there were some people who insisted that the last word should be read as "cooks."

"Ridiculous," said the king. "What is found in cooks, pray? Nothing at all. There can be no connection between cooks and my daughter." And he went on with his neat timetables ruled in red ink, with spaces for Latin, trigonometry, and political economy.

From the age of five poor Griselda was stuffed with these subjects, and she hated them all equally. In Latin she could only remember such phrases as "Give the boy the bread" and "Each of the soldiers carried his own food." In mathematics she could only work out the sort of problems in which two men have to pick a given quantity of apples, working at different speeds.

When she was twelve she could stand it no longer, and she went to her father and begged him to let her give up her education and learn cooking.

"Learn cooking?" said he king, horrified. "Remember you will have to earn your living when we are gone. You won't come into a kingdom like your brother. Do you propose to be a cook, may I ask?"

"Yes," said Griselda.

"Don't you think it will look rather odd in the advertisements? H. R. H. Griselda. Good plain cooking. Omelettes a specialty. I must say, I should have thought that a daughter of mine could select a better career."

However, Griselda had made up her mind, and finally she was allowed to learn cooking in the palace kitchen.

Presently the king and queen became old and died, and Griselda's brother Florizel came to the throne. He was very fond of Griselda and begged her to stay with him, but she decided that the time had come for her to seek her fortune, so she set off one night, secretly and in disguise, in order to avoid any further persuasions and bother. She asked an obliging fisherman to take her across the sea in his boat, and he left her the next morning, alone, but not in the least downhearted, on a foreign shore.

Some lobster gatherers met her there and asked her who she was.

"I'm a princess," she said absently.

"Go on," they cried, laughing, though not unkindly, at her black boot-button eyes and shiny red cheeks.

"I mean I'm a cook," she amended.

"That's a bit more like it. Over here for the competition, are you? You'll find the palace, third turning on the right down the road."

Griselda had no idea what they were talking about, but she followed their directions and soon came to a handsome palace. There was a notice on the gate which read:

Cooks!

Grand Competition!

The winner of this competition will receive the post of chief cook to the palace together with half the kingdom (if male) or His Majesty's hand and heart in marriage (if female).

Further particulars within.

Griselda went inside and found that the competition was just about to begin. Hundreds of cooks were already lined up in the vast, spotless palace kitchen, where all the cooking utensils were of silver, and the dishes of gold.

A pale, anxious-looking young man was running around dealing out numbers to the competitors. He gave Griselda a number on a piece of paper and pushed her into line. She could hear him saying: "Oh mercy me, whatever shall I do about supper if none of them come up to standard?"

"Is that the king?" Griselda asked in surprise.

"Hush, they're going to begin. Yes, it is."

The first event was an apple-peeling competition, which Griselda won easily by peeling twenty point four apples in three minutes. Next she won the obstacle race, in which competitors had to go over a complicated course, carrying two eggs in one hand and a frying pan in the other, and finish by making an omelette. She then won two more events in quick succession — the *Good Housewife Test* (which entailed making a nourishing stew out of an old boot and a cabbage leaf), and the *Discrimination Test* (distinguishing between butter and marge with her eyes shut).

There began to be some muttering among the other competitors, which increased as she went on with a string of successes. She made a delicious meal from two leftover sardines and some cold porridge. Her spongecake was so light that when the king opened his mouth to taste it, he blew it out of the window. Her bread rose till it burst the oven. She tossed her pancake three times as high as any of the others, and sprinkled it with sugar and lemon as it fell. In fact there was no doubt that she was the "Queen of the Cooks", and the king was quite exhausted and pale with excitement by the end of the competition, at having found such a treasure.

"I think we all agree," he announced, "that Miss — er — that Number 555 has won this contest, and I have much pleasure — "

However, his voice at this point was drowned by the hoarse outcry from the other angry and disappointed competitors, and it looked as if there were going to be a riot. One of the rejected spongecakes was flung at Griselda, but it was so heavy that it only got halfway across the room.

The disturbance did not last long, for the king, knowing that cooks generally have hot tempers, had ordered the palace militia to be on guard outside, and all the unsuccessful candidates were soon bundled out of doors.

"In short," said the king, finishing, "I have pleasure in offering you the job of palace cook."

"And I have pleasure in accepting it," said Griselda, curt-sying.

"As well as my hand and heart in marriage," he pursued.

"No, thank you."

"I beg your pardon?"

"It's very kind of you," said Griselda, "but I wouldn't feel inclined to marry someone just because he liked my cooking."

"But it was a clause of the competition," said the king, outraged.

"Never mind."

"And then there was a prophecy about it."

"Oh dear, another prophecy?" said Griselda, who felt that one in her life had been enough nuisance.

"It said:

The girl who weds our king so gay and gallant
Will be a cook of most uncommon talent.

And you can't deny that you are one, can you?"

Griselda couldn't but she did feel that "gay and gallant" hardly described the pale, anxious young creature who stood before her.

"And if you don't marry me you might leave at any time, and then what should I do about my meals?" he said miserably. "The last cook used to make the cream sauce with corn starch."

"Well, if you don't stop bothering me I certainly shall leave, right away," said Griselda briskly, "so run along now, out of my kitchen, or I shall never have dinner ready." And she shooed him out.

She found that he was a terrible fusser, and always popping into the kitchen to ask if she was sure she had put enough salt in the pastry, or if the oven was hot enough. She found that she was able to manage him, however, for the threat of leaving always quieted him down at once, and things soon settled very comfortably.

But enemies were at work.

The unsuccessful candidates had banded themselves together in order to get Griselda out of favor. They lurked about the palace in disguise, and took every opportunity of laying obstacles in the way of her work. They sprinkled weed killer over the parsley in the gardens when they heard the king ask for parsley sauce, bought up all the rice in the kingdom if he wanted rice pudding, and substituted salt for sugar and cement for flour when Griselda's back was turned.

Griselda, however, was never at a loss. She had with her *Mrs Beeton's Palace Cookery*, and in the chapter on "Cookery During Wars and Revolutions" she found recipes for *Rice Pudding Without Using Rice* and many other equally convenient hints and suggestions which helped her to defeat the conspirators.

They soon found that their tactics were useless, and resolved upon bolder measures. They went to the witch in the nearby wood and asked her to get rid of Griselda for them — expense no object.

"Griselda," said the witch thoughtfully. "I wonder if that would be the baby I had to uglify about twenty years ago? What would you like me to do with her?"

"We thought you might send her to the dragon in the desert."

"Yes, that would do very well. I seem to remember that there's some prophecy —

When the dragon feels saddish,
Feed him on a radish.

— but I doubt if there's much chance of her knowing that,
and it doesn't say what would happen if she did. Very well,
you may take it as settled. That will be ten and six, please."

At that very instant a black, magic cloud swept down on
Griselda as she stood making a salad, and carried her into
the middle of the desert where the dragon lived. She was
rather annoyed, but put a good face on it, and at once began
looking for an oasis.

After a couple of hours of walking through sand she came
within sight of some palm trees, but was depressed to see the
dragon there too, lying in the shade — a vast, green and gold
monster.

"Still," she thought, "there's room for us both. If I don't
annoy him, perhaps he won't annoy me."

And walking up, she nodded to him politely, said
"Excuse me," and took a drink at the spring. The dragon
took no notice at all.

During the next three or four days, Griselda, who was a
sociable creature, found that the dragon enjoyed being read
aloud to. He stretched himself out comfortably with his nose
on his claws, and seemed to take a lively interest in *Palace
Cookery*, which was the only book she had with her. During
their simple meals of dates he often looked hopefully at the
book, and sometimes pushed it toward her with the tip of his
tail, as if asking for more. In fact, they grew most attached to
each other, and Griselda often thought how she would miss
him if she were rescued.

One afternoon she had been reading the chapter on

"Magic Foods, and How to Deal with Culinary Spells" when she looked up to see that the dragon was crying bitterly.

"Why, dragon!" she exclaimed, "don't take on so. Whatever is the matter?"

Feeling in her apron pocket for a knob of sugar or something to comfort him, she found a radish, left over from her last salad.

"Here," she said, holding it out, "chew this up — it'll make you feel better."

Meanwhile at home the young king was having a horrible time. When Griselda vanished, he hired first one, then others, of the wicked conspirators, but they were such bad cooks that he discharged them all, and was finally reduced to living on eggs, which he boiled himself. His health was shattered, and the affairs of the kingdom were in frightful disorder.

He was sitting down to his egg one day, in gloom, when in walked Griselda, looking very brown.

"My goodness!" he exclaimed, jumping up. "I am glad to see you. They told me you had been eaten by a dragon. Now we can have some decent meals again."

"Well, I must say, I think you might have sent a rescue force or something," said Griselda with spirit. "However, as it happens it all turned out for the best. Look who's with me."

Behind her there was a handsome young man, who came forward and said cheerfully, "I don't expect you remember me, but I'm your elder brother."

"Not the one that was stolen by the wicked enchanter?"

"That's right. He turned me into a dragon, and Griselda rescued me with a radish."

"Well, that is a relief," said the king happily. "I was so

tired of being king, you can't think. Now you can do all that, and I can live with you in the palace and eat Griselda's wonderful food."

"Do you mind his living with us?" asked the new king, turning to Griselda. "By the way," he added, "Griselda and I are married."

"Of course I don't mind," said Griselda. "I'll go and start making supper right away, and you can both come and peel the potatoes."

So they all lived happily ever after. Griselda stayed very plain, but nobody minded.

The Lilac in the Lake

———•———

There was this old boy, Enoch Dibben, the schoolmaster at a little place at the back of beyond, Grydale, it's called, likely you'll not have heard of it. The lads at that village are terrible teasers to a boy; sure as one of them looks you in the eye, it's because he's dropped a live eel in your lunch bucket, or loosed a sackful of grasshoppers inside your car, or tied your shoelaces together so that you'll fall over when you try to walk. Teasers, and artful, they are, but not an ounce of vice in them. Indeed, Mr Dibben rather enjoyed their goings on. He was such a dreamy old fellow, wandering about the dale with his hands behind his back and his head in the clouds, that it was somewhere pleasant for him to feel folk noticed he was there to the extent of filling his inkwell with golden syrup, as Charlie Herdman did one Friday afternoon. For he was a single man, and sometimes felt a bit lonely, with no one to warm his slippers or fry his bacon, or bake him a bit of parkin for a Sunday treat.

It's a quiet little place, Grydale, thirty miles from the

nearest railway. Up above it on each side the fells climb out of sight. After the sun goes down you can hear a pheasant cluck in Grassy Woods, five miles off, or a dog barking in Shipton, down at the foot of the valley.

Sometimes at night in his little stone cottage, Mr Dibben, snug in bed, would think he heard a tapping at the door. Specially on a milky summer night, when you could hardly tell if the noise that broke the silence was the stream whispering or your own heart beating, he used to think somebody quietly knocked at his door; he used to think he could hear-voices calling: "Mr Dibben! Mr Dibben! Please come down and let us in! We're so lonely and cold! Let us in, and we'll cook for you and clean for you, we'll dig your garden and darn your socks, we'll wash your shirts and tidy your papers and bake your bread and sharpen your pencils!"

Mr Dibben, though, took no notice of this, except maybe to burrow deeper in the bedclothes. "It's those naughty boys, he would think," shutting his eyes tight; "they want me to come down and open the door; then a bucket of potato peelings will probably fall on my head while they run off up to the village laughing themselves into hiccups. I'm not such a fool as that!"

Sometimes of a morning when he opened his eyes and the blue day came rushing in he'd wonder if he had dreamed the voices; sometimes he'd resolve that next time he heard them he'd go down to the door and open it. But somehow he never did.

There were only three cars in Grydale; Mr Dibben's old Rattler was one of them The boys left his car alone, whatever else they did, they never played any of their tricks on Rattler; when you live so cut off you get to treat cars with respect. So,

on fine weekends and summer evenings, Mr Dibben was a
great wanderer, and you might come across him anywhere
about the countryside from Mickle Fell to Spurn Head.

What was he doing? Hunting for legends. If he heard tell
of a village where they'd a bewitched bake-house, or where
the hares danced in a ring on Midsummer Eve, or where the
ghost of King Richard sat eating gooseberries in the church-
yard, first free moment Mr Dibben had he'd be off, fast as
old Rattler could make it at a galloping eighteen miles an
hour. And once there he'd get the whole tale out of the oldest inhabitant — or the youngest — or whoever had a fancy
to sit in the sun spinning tall tales.

Mr Dibben wrote them all down on sheets of paper with
holes at one side and stuck them in a book. Bigger than the
Bible it would be, when finished, and he was that proud of it.
"When it's published," he used to say, "my name will be
known throughout the length and breadth of England." But
there were some in the village used to think he'd better get a
move on, sending it to a publisher, or one of these days he'd
find himself knocking at St. Peter's gate with all his bits of
paper still under his arm. And no one's yet said if they publish
books in heaven. Though most likely they do, or what should
we all do for a read on a sunny afternoon in the fields of Eden?

There's a many stories in our countryside; one grows out
of another as quick as groundsel. If a farmer has a dog that's
trained to answer the phone, or someone's house falls down
because the builder forgot the mortar, or a boggart sits with
the family in the evenings, playing Scrabble and forecasting
the winner of the Derby, you may be sure the news will get all
over the village in a twinkling, and from there, embroidered
up a bit, to the four corners of the county, even as far away as
Nottingham.

So Mr Dibben was well occupied, chasing far and wide like a pup after bumblebees, and it wasn't till he'd been in Grydale nigh on ten year that he found, with all his questings and questionings, he'd clean missed one of the best tales of all, and that on his own doorstep: the tale of the Grydale Singers.

Charlie Herdman told it to him then, one hot sleepy afternoon after school. Charlie had a reason for this: He wanted to keep Mr Dibben distracted and out of the way up in the schoolhouse while some friends of his prepared a little surprise. So he said to the old boy, as they were tidying up the infants' books (Charlie was monitor that week): "I wonder you aren't afeared to live in that house of yourn, all on your own down below the village, Master Dibben. Don't you never think the Grydale Singers might spirit you away?"

"Grydale Singers?" says Mr Dibben, all agog at once. "What are they? Grydale Singers, I don't believe I've ever heard of them. Leave rubbing the blackboard, my boy — I'll do that — now you tell me about these Grydale Singers." And he commences rubbing the board with his handkerchief.

"Well," artful Charlie says, thoroughly enjoying himself now, "it's a tale we have in the village about these seven sisters who lived here in my grandfather's time, or it may have been in his granfer's time, I ain't so special sure, but it was in the days when folk rode horseback and the summers was always hot and mushrooms grew on the village green and lasses wore their hair hanging long and loose down their backs."

"Seven sisters — yes, yes," Mr Dibben he says. "Just a minute Charlie, while I give the tape recorder a bit of a bang — it's stuck again."

For Mr Dibben had this tape recorder he used for taking down the stories he collected, and also for teaching the children in school and trying to make them say their a's long and droopy, like an old bellwether, instead of short and crisp like a snapped stick. He'd bought it secondhand in Leeds and tinkered about with it till it worked well enough, but times it was a bit temperamental and when he played it back instead of the voice you expected it would give you a bit of the Shipton Orpheus Choir's rendering of "For unto us a child is born" or the frogs croaking in Mallam Tarn.

"Right, Charlie, I've got it going again — now tell us about those seven sisters. What were their names?"

"Why," Charlie says, "there's some believe it wasn't seven sisters but three, or maybe four, but the way I heard it there's seven of 'em, and their names were Mary, Mercy, Marila, Martha, Marian, Marjorie, and Marigold, and they was the blacksmith's lasses, Mr Artingstall it was then, and pretty as a podful of young peas. Fair hair, blue eyes, and all that. Half the lads in the village was after them. They lived in the blacksmith's cottage, that's the one you have now, Mr Dibben, afore my granda's grandad bought it up, and they used to help their dad with blowing the bellows and such-like. Pretty as they were, they was that uppish and stan-doffish they'd sworn none of them 'ud ever marry, not a one of them could abide the male sex. Spinsters to their deathbeds they declared they'd be, on account of all the teasing they'd gone through at school, the lads in Grydale — as you know — being fond of a lark."

"Seven sisters sworn not to marry — yes, yes," Mr Dibben says, setting light to the blackboard rubber instead of his pipe. "This is most interesting, Charlie, go on. What happened to them?"

"They used to sing a lot — any party or wedding, funeral

or christening there was in the village the Artingstall lasses would be on hand obliging with a bit of Stainer or whatever was suitable. And of an evening they'd sit under the lilac bush in the garden — the same one that's still there now, Mr Dibben — singing away like a sipkin of thrushes.

Well, about the time Mary, that's the eldest one, was getting on for twenty-three and folk had started to think maybe they'd stick to their word and really would end up as old maids, people began to notice that when they sang a chorus, one of 'em was always flat. And next thing they found was that Mary had been secretly running off to meet a young fellow, name of Huxtable, kind of a wandering peddler who came up to the village once a month with ribbons and saucepans, and next thing was, he and Mary got wed. Well, the other sisters put a good face on it, they sang at her wedding, but they felt she'd let the family down, they swore they'd never do such a thing. In fact it made them more set against men than ever, they reckoned Huxtable had fair bewitched her. I forget whether he took her to Scunthorpe or Skegness or Scarborough for the honeymoon, but anyhow, not long after they got back they went out one day fishing on Grydale Water, in a rowboat, and Mary somehow got her long hair caught in the anchor chain, was pulled overboard with it, down to the bottom, and drowned. Her husband was fair mazed with grief, some say he jumped right overboard after her and that was the end of him, others that he joined the French Foreign Legion and was seen in Whitby twenty years after, declaring that he was the Emperor Boneypart. Anyway, he never came back to Grydale."

"What became of the other sisters?"

"The very night after she was drowned they went out to

the lilac tree for the last time and sang a lament for her, folk who heard it said it was so sad that the owls in the church-yard elms were boohooing too, and the lilac tree dropped all its blossom for pity. And when they'd done, they all got up and walked into Grydale Water and that was the end of them."

"Really?" says Mr Dibben, absent-mindedly putting his ball-point in his mouth and his lighted pipe in his pocket. "Dear me, what a remarkable tale. Is that the end of it, Charlie?"

"Not quite," Charlie says. "For there's folk as says that from that day to this, every night from half past eleven to twelve midnight, those sisters can be heard under the lilac tree singing their lament — only they won't do it if there's a man within earshot because they're still fell set against the whole flaysome race. It's said they'll go on lamenting till trout swim in Grassy Wood, or till a man can be found that'll walk into Grydale Water for love of them."

"Dear me," Mr Dibben said again. "So they won't sing when a man's about? Are there ladies in the village that have heard them, then?"

"My mam' says she has, many a time," Charlie says. "When she's been coming home late from the Ladies' Glee Club or the bingo drive."

"I must go and see your good mother without delay," says Mr Dibben, trying to lock up his desk with a bit of black-board chalk.

Before he left he gave Charlie a present — a pencil case it was, made of red-painted tin and shaped like a rocket. When you twisted the bottom round, strips of numbers up the side worked out the multiplication table for you, all the way from

1 × 1 to 9 × 9 . "That's for you, Charlie my boy, as a reward
for such an exceedingly interesting piece of lore."

"No, no, Mr Dibben, I don't want anything, honest I
don't!"

Charlie was a bit upset at being given a present, and such
a handsome one too. But Mr Dibben insisted, and then hurried off to ask all the womenfolk in the village if they'd ever
heard the Grydale Singers. Some said yes, some said no,
some said they didn't believe in such foolishness. Time Mr
Dibben went home it was getting toward dusk, the swifts
had stopped scooping for flies and gone to roost in the
eaves.

He opened his gate, gave a bit of a glance at the historic
lilac bush, never noticed the hedge, which heaved and shook
with giggles because half the boys of the village were lodged
in it, and went on to open his front door, which led straight
into the little parlor. He found the door uncommonly hard
to shift, and when at last he got it open, about a ton of water
rushed out at him. The boys had been busy ever since
school finished, filling his room full of river through a hose
pipe led from Grydale Falls. Mr Dibben's cottage, the only
house below the falls, was well downhill from the village, so
it was easy enough to do.

The old chap wasn't angry about it, only astonished. He
stood scratching his head, while the water pushed past him
down the garden path like brown coffee suds.

"Dear have mercy!" says he to himself. "Can I have left
the kitchen tap on?"

So like an old puzzled bird he looked, as he stood there
on one leg, scratching his head, an old bird with its feathers
all ruffled up, that the boys, who were as good-natured a set

of young addlepates as you could hope to find, hadn't the heart to leave him to clear up the mess. They came bursting out of the hedge, half choked with laughing, patted Mr Dibben, picked him up, carried him into his kitchen, which was still dry, and started mopping down the parlor floor.

"Eh, dear, Mr Dibben, didn't you ever guess?" Charlie said to him. "Didn't you wonder why I was keeping you so long at the school?"

"But then, that story you told me about the singers — was not that a true tale, Charlie?"

"The Grydale Singers? Yes, that was a canty tale enough," Charlie told him. "I daresay they'd be singing away now if we wasn't about."

Relieved to hear this, which was the only thing that had worried him, Mr Dibben went to his bed, leaving the boys to get on with swabbing down the parlor. Next day the place was still damp enough and he thought it right to go along to Farmer Herdman, who was his landlord, and explain what had happened. Farmer Herdman shook his head over the tale (though he couldn't forbear a grin, having been a toy himself once) and offered to give them all a dusting if Mr Dibben wished. But the old boy shook his head.

"I don't hold it agen' them," he says. "Young blood will out. I only thought fit to mention it, Mr Herdman, to explain how the house came to be so uncommon damp."

"As to that," Farmer Herdman he says, "the house'll be damper still soon enough. I was going to come and see you, Master Dibben, about that very thing."

Then he began explaining something about the new dam at Shipton to the schoolmaster, who didn't hear a single word he said. For a grand notion had just come into Mr Dibben's head: Why not try to get a recording of the Grydale Singers on his tape machine? Likely enough the young ladies had never heard of a tape recorder and would have no suspicions of it, might not even notice it quietly spinning away, if he hid it under the grass and leaves. And if they did happen to spot it — well, a tape recorder's not the same as a man, is it, no reason why that should stop them singing? As you might imagine, Mr Dibben, who used to sing himself when he was young, baritone in the Bottlewell Male Voice Choir, was mortal keen to be the first man to hear these poor sorrowful singers, and he thought he had hit on the very answer to the problem. The only snag was that he himself would have to clear out for a night and go well away so that his presence wouldn't put a cramp in the business. Where could he go? he wondered, and then he remembered his Auntie Sarah in York. She would put him up, and willing.

"So do you want to see about getting the furniture shifted, or will you leave it to me?" says Farmer Herdman, finishing his long explanation, and Mr Dibben, who hadn't taken in a word of it, quickly says, "Oh, I will, I'll look after it, thank'ee," for he didn't want anybody meddling around the cottage while he was away and maybe upsetting the Singers. He put his hat on inside out, and bustled off home to pack up a few things.

Late that night, about twenty past eleven, he set off, first hiding the tape recorder under the lilac tree in a clump of fern where he hoped the ghostly sisters wouldn't notice it. The tape was a two-hour one, so he calculated there would be enough and to spare for recording the lament.

Away he drove, along the side of the valley, past Grydale Water, glimmering in the hazy moonlight, and made his way to York city, where, as it chanced, he found his Auntie Sarah on her deathbed, and not before it was time either, since she was nigh on a hundred.

"Don't forget to wind the clock when I'm gone, Enoch Dibben," she croaked at him. "I've left you all my money, Enoch, on condition you have this house turned into a cats' home. Now I must be on my way — I'm ten minutes late already. My old-crony Nancy Thorpe is waiting for me up there in Paradise; I promised to take her all the latest knitting patterns," and with that she took and died. Mr Dibben was a bit put out, since he was now obliged to stay in York, make arrangements for the funeral, see to moving the pusses into their new home, not to mention winding the clock. A fortnight it took him getting everything straight, and a marble slab for Auntie Sarah with half a cherub on it. He was in a fret, too, about how his tape recorder was standing the weather, though to be sure he'd left it in a waterproof cover.

Soon as the cats were in, and a caretaker to feed them and wind the clock, he was off, hotfoot, back to Grydale, where things had not been standing still, as you shall hear.

It was late night again when Mr Dibben drove back up the daleside; the mist stood in the bottom of the valley like clumps of thistledown, and the night was so quiet that old Rattler's chug-chug sounded louder than cannon fire. Mr Dibben felt a bit lonesome thinking of the cats all snug together in their new home, and Auntie Sarah so cozy up in Paradise a-chatting with Mrs Thorpe over their "plain-and-pearl," while he had only his cold empty cottage waiting for him.

When he reached the track turning down off the main road to his own house he was a bit perplexed because there seemed to be water across the road, though with all the mist lying it was hard to be sure.

"Dang it," says Mr Dibben, "are my eyes deceiving me? Surely to gracious the lake can't have risen all that much? There's not been a drop of rain in York for the last fortnight. Can it be those boys up to their tricks again?"

He stopped Rattler in the middle of the track, got out, and ambled forward on foot.

"My eyes must be deceiving me," he says then. "It must be some kind of mirage. Because if the water is up here, where I think I see it, then my house is under the lake up to the chimney pots — which is out of the question. For if my house is under water up to the chimneys, then my tape recorder would be under water also — which is not to be thought of. I am having a hallucination," he says, "but I will ignore it."

On he goes, up to his ankles first, then up to his knees. Then he was wading with his belt under water, then his chin was covered, and at last Mr Dibben was clean gone under the water, plodding forward in search of this tape recorder, and naught left visible but a trail of bubbles.

Well! When he got to his front gate a perfect chorus of voices greeted him.

"Evening, Mr Dibben!"

"Welcome home, then, Mr Dibben!"

"We've got your slippers a-warming, Mr Dibben!"

"And a pot of tea mashed!"

"And a rasher of bacon frying!"

"And a lovely bit of parkin in the oven!"

"And the best cheesecakes and marmalade this side of Doncaster!"

Then they all said together: "Oh, Mr Dibben, we're so pleased you've come home!"

Mr Dibben was fair bewildered, as you can imagine, by such a welcome, but he couldn't help being pleased too, not a doubt of that. It was plain that the Artingstall lasses had grown tired of their solitary life and wanted someone to take care of. The only thing that worried him was, what had become of his recording of the lament, under all that lake water, but Mercy Artingstall told him, "To tell you the truth, Mr Dibben, we was so cast down and low-spirited the night we thought you'd gone off and left us, that we never sang a note. But, she says, "we'll make up for that now!"

Of course, next day in Grydale village they was fair upset to find Mr Dibben's old Rattler standing on the edge of the new reservoir, and him nowhere to be seen.

"I blame myself, that I do!" says Farmer Herdman. "I should have made certain sure that he knew about the dam they was building at valley-foot, and how the reservoir would cover his cottage. I should have moved his furniture myself into the new little house I had ready for him up in the village. I ought to have remembered what an absentminded old chap he was. I'm right downhearted, and that's the truth."

As for Charlie Herdman, he went about the place with a face as long as an eight-day clock, and declared he'd keep the red tin pencil case all his life in memory of poor Mr Dibben. And Farmer Herdman said he'd have the book of tales (which they found in old Rattler) printed up in big print, with fine colored pictures, at his own expense as a memorial.

But they needn't have worried about keeping Mr Dibben's memory green. Punctual that night at half past eleven, the Grydale Singers started up over the lake, over the lilac bush that was now drowned eighteen foot deep in Grydale Water — and this time they'd a baritone with them as well. And no nonsense about not singing if there was men within earshot — the noise they made, with a rousing good rendering of the Hallelujah Chorus, was enough to fetch the whole village out of its beds, and it was the same each night after and ever since.

In fact, though there's no denying it draws the tourist business (coaches come from as far afield as Hull) some of the folk in Grydale are beginning to grumble about the nightly choruses, and have even written to the County Council to complain.

But the council says that nothing can be done.

A Harp of Fishbones

———•———

Little Nerryn lived in the half-ruined mill at the upper end of
the village, where the stream ran out of the forest. The old
miller's name was Timorash, but she called him uncle. Her
own father and mother were dead, long before she could
remember. Timorash was no real kin, nor was he particularly kind to her; he was a lazy old man. He never troubled
to grow corn as the other people in the village did in little
patches in the clearing below the village before the forest
began again. When people brought him corn to grind he
took one-fifth of it as his fee and this, with wild plums which
Nerryn gathered and dried, and carp from the deep millpool, kept him and the child fed through the short bright
summers and the long silent winters.

Nerryn learned to do the cooking when she was seven or
eight; she toasted fish on sticks over the fire and baked cakes
of bread on a flat stone; Timorash beat her if the food was
burnt, but it mostly was, just the same, because so often half
her mind would be elsewhere, listening to the bell-like call of

a bird or pondering about what made the difference between the stream's voice in winter and in summer. When she was a little older Timorash taught her how to work the mill, opening the sluice-gate so that the green, clear mountain water could hurl down against the great wooden paddle-wheel. Nerryn liked this much better, since she had already spent hours watching the stream endlessly pouring and plaiting down its narrow passage. Old Timorash had hoped that now he would be able to give up work altogether and lie in the sun all day, or crouch by the fire, slowly adding one stick after another and dreaming about barley wine. But Nerryn forgot to take flour in payment from the villagers, who were in no hurry to remind her, so the old man angrily decided that this plan would not answer, and sent her out to work.

First she worked for one household, then for another.

The people of the village had come from the plains; they were surly, big-boned, and lank, with tow-coloured hair and pale eyes; even the children seldom spoke. Little Nerryn some-times wondered, looking at her reflection in the millpool, how it was that she should be so different from them, small and brown-skinned, with dark hair like a bird's feathers and hazelnut eyes. But it was no use asking questions of old Timorash, who never answered except by grunting or throwing a clod of earth at her. Another difference was that she loved to chatter, and this was perhaps the main reason why the people she worked for soon sent her packing.

There were other reasons too, for, though Nerryn was willing enough to work, things often distracted her.

"She let the bread burn while she ran outside to listen to a curlew," said one.

"When she was helping me cut the hay she asked so

many questions that my ears have ached for three days,"
complained another.

"Instead of scaring off the birds from my corn-patch she
sat with her chin on her fists, watching them gobble down half
a winter's supply and whistling to them!" grumbled a third.

Nobody would keep her more than a few days, and she
had plenty of beatings, especially from Timorash, who had
hoped that her earnings would pay for a keg of barley wine.
Once in his life he had had a whole keg, and he still felt
angry when he remembered that it was finished.

At last Nerryn went to work for an old woman who lived
in a tumbledown hut at the bottom of the street. Her name
was Saroon and she was by far the oldest in the village, so
withered and wrinkled that most people thought she was a
witch; besides, she knew when it was going to rain and was
the only person in the place who did not fear to venture a little way into the forest. But she was growing weak now, and
stiff, and wanted somebody to help dig her corn-patch and
cut wood. Nevertheless she hardly seemed to welcome help
when it came. As Nerryn moved about at the tasks she was
set, the old woman's little red-rimmed eyes followed her sus-
piciously; she hobbled round the hut watching through
cracks, grumbling and chuntering to herself, never losing
sight of the girl for a moment, like some cross-grained old
animal that sees a stranger near its burrow.

On the fourth day she said,

"You're singing, girl."

"I — I'm sorry," Nerryn stammered. "I didn't mean to —
I wasn't thinking. Don't beat me, please."

"Humph," said the old woman, but she did not beat Nerryn that time. And next day, watching through the window-
hole while Nerryn chopped wood, she said,

"You're not singing."

Nerryn jumped. She had not known the old woman was so near.

"I thought you didn't like me to," she faltered.

"I didn't say so, did I?"

Muttering, the old woman stumped off to the back of the hut and began to sort through a box of mildewy nuts. "As if I should care," Nerryn heard her grumble, "whether the girl sings or not!" But next day she put her head out of the door, while Nerryn hoed the corn-patch, and said, "sing, child!"

Nerryn looked at her, doubtful and timid, to see if she really meant it, but she nodded her head energetically, till the tangled grey locks jounced on her shoulders, and repeated, "Sing!"

So presently the clear, tiny thread of Nerryn's song began again as she sliced off the weeds; and old Saroon came out and sat on an upturned log beside the door, pounding roots for soup and mumbling to herself in time to the sound. And at the end of the week she did not dismiss the girl, as everyone else had done, though what she paid was so little that Timorash grumbled every time Nerryn brought it home. At this rate twenty years would go by before he had saved enough for a keg of barley wine.

One day Saroon said,

"Your father used to sing."

This was the first time anyone had spoken of him.

"Oh," Nerryn cried, forgetting her fear of the old woman. "Tell me about him."

"Why should I?" old Saroon said sourly. "He never did anything for *me*." And she hobbled off to fetch a pot of water. But later she relented and said,

"His hair was the colour of ash buds, like yours. And he carried a harp."

"A harp, what is a harp?"

"Oh, don't pester, child. I'm busy."

But another day she said, "A harp is a thing to make music. His was a gold one, but it was broken."

"Gold, what is gold?"

"This," said the old woman, and she pulled out a small, thin disc which she wore on a cord of plaited grass around her neck.

"Why!" Nerryn exclaimed. "Everybody in the village has one of those except Timorash and me. I've often asked what they were but no one would answer."

"They are gold. When your father went off and left you and the harp with Timorash, the old man ground up the harp between the millstones. And he melted down the gold powder and made it into these little circles and sold them to everybody in the village, and bought a keg of barley wine. He told us they would bring good luck. But I have never had any good luck and that was a long time ago. And Timorash has long since drunk all his barley wine."

"Where did my father go?" asked Nerryn.

"Into the forest," the old woman snapped. "I could have told him he was in for trouble. I could have warned him. But he never asked *my* advice."

She sniffed, and set a pot of herbs boiling on the fire. And Nerryn could get no more out of her that day.

But little by little, as time passed, more came out.

"Your father came from over the mountains. High up yonder, he said, there was a great city, with houses and palaces and temples, and as many rich people as there are fish in the millpool. Best of all, there was always music playing in the streets and houses and in the temples. But then the goddess of the mountain became angry, and fire burst out of a crack in the hillside. And then a great cold came, so that people froze where they stood. Your father said he only just managed to escape with you by running very fast. Your mother had died in the fire."

"Where was he going?"

"The king of the city had ordered him to go for help."

"What sort of help?"

"Don't ask *me*," the old woman grumbled. "You'd think he'd have settled down here like a person of sense, and mended his harp. But no, on he must go, leaving you behind so that he could travel faster. He said he'd fetch you again on his way back. But of course he never did come back — one day I found his bones in the forest. The birds must have killed him."

"How do you *know* they were my father's bones?"

"Because of the tablet he carried. See, here it is, with his name on it, Heramon the harper."

"Tell me more about the harp!"

"It was shaped like this," the old woman said. They were washing clothes by the stream, and she drew with her finger in the mud. "Like this, and it had golden strings across, so. All but one of the strings had melted in the fire from the mountain. Even on just one string he could make very beautiful music, that would force you to stop whatever you were doing and listen. It is a pity he had to leave the harp behind. Timorash wanted it as payment for looking after you. If your father had taken the harp with him, perhaps he would have been able to reach the other side of the forest."

Nerryn thought about this story a great deal. For the next
few weeks she did even less work than usual and was mostly
to be found squatting with her chin on her fists by the side
of the stream. Saroon beat her, but not very hard. Then one
day Nerryn said,

"I shall make a harp."

"Hah!" sniffed the old woman. "You! What do you know
of such things?"

After a few minutes she asked,

"What will you make it from?"

Nerryn said, "I shall make it of fishbones. Some of the
biggest carp in the millpool have bones as thick as my wrist,
and they are very strong."

"Timorash will never allow it."

"I shall wait till he is asleep, then."

So Nerryn waited till night, and then she took a chunk of
rotten wood, which glows in the dark, and dived into the
deep millpool, swimming down and down to the depths
where the biggest carp lurk, among the mud and weeds and
old sunken logs.

When they saw the glimmer of the wood through the
water, all the fish came nosing and nibbling and swimming
round Nerryn, curious to find if this thing which shone so
strangely was good to eat. She waited as long as she could
bear it, holding her breath, till a great barrel-shaped monster
slid nudging right up against her; then, quick as a flash, she
wrapped her arms round his slippery sides and fled up with
a bursting heart to the surface.

Much to her surprise, old Saroon was there, waiting in the
dark on the bank. But the old woman only said,

"You had better bring the carp to my hut. After all, you

want no more than the bones, and it would be a pity to waste all the good meat. I can live on it for a week." So she cut the meat off the bones, which were coal-black but had a sheen on them like mother-of-pearl. Nerryn dried them by the fire, and then she joined together the three biggest, notching them to fit, and cementing them with a glue which she made by boiling some of the smaller bones together. She used long, thin, strong bones for strings, joining them to the frame in the same manner.

All the time old Saroon watched closely. Sometimes she would say,

"That was not the way of it. Heramon's harp was wider," or "You are putting the strings too far apart. There should be more of them, and they should be tighter."

When at last it was done, she said,

"Now you must hang it in the sun to dry."

So for three days the harp hung drying in the sun and wind. At night Saroon took it into her hut and covered it with a cloth. On the fourth day she said,

"Now, play!"

Nerryn rubbed her finger across the strings, and they gave out a liquid murmur, like that of a stream running over pebbles, under a bridge. She plucked a string, and the noise was like that a drop of water makes, falling in a hollow place.

"That will be music," old Saroon said, nodding her head, satisfied. "It is not quite the same as the sound from your father's harp, but it is music. Now you shall play me tunes every day, and I shall sit in the sun and listen."

"No," said Nerryn, "for if Timorash hears me playing he will take the harp away and break it or sell it. I shall go to my father's city and see if I can find any of his kin there."

At this old Saroon was very angry. "Here have I taken all these pains to help you, and what reward do I get for it? How much pleasure do you think I have, living among dolts in this dismal place? I was not born here, any more than you were. You could at least play to me at night, when Timorash is asleep."

"Well, I will play to you for seven nights," Nerryn said.

Each night old Saroon tried to persuade her not to go, and she tried harder as Nerryn became more skilful in playing, and drew from the fishbone harp a curious watery music, like the songs that birds sing when it is raining. But Nerryn would not be persuaded to stay, and when she saw this, on the seventh night, Saroon said, "I suppose I shall have to tell you how to go through the forest. Otherwise you will certainly die, as your father did. When you go among the trees you will find that the grass underfoot is thick and strong and hairy, and the farther you go, the higher it grows, as high as your waist. And it is sticky and clings to you, so that you can only go forward slowly, one step at a time. Then, in the middle of the forest, perched in the branches, are vultures who will drop on you and peck you to death if you stand still for more than a minute."

"How do you know all this?" Nerryn said.

"I have tried many times to go through the forest, but it is too far for me; I grow tired and have to turn back. The vultures take no notice of me, I am too old and withered, but a tender young piece like you would be just what they fancy."

"Then what must I do?" Nerryn asked.

"You must play music on your harp till they fall asleep; then, while they sleep, cut the grass with your knife and go forward as fast as you can."

Nerryn said, "If I cut you enough fuel for a month, and catch you another carp, and gather you a bushel of nuts, will you give me your little gold circle, or my father's tablet?"

But this Saroon would not do. She did, though, break off the corner of the tablet which had Heramon the Harare's name on it, and give that to Nerryn.

"But don't blame me," she said sourly, "if you find the city all burnt and frozen, with not a living soul to walk its streets."

"Oh, it will all have been rebuilt by this time," Nerryn said. "I shall find my father's people, or my mother's, and I shall come back for you, riding a white mule and leading another."

"Fairy tales!" old Saroon said angrily. "Be off with you, then. If you don't wish to stay I'm sure I don't want you idling about the place. All the work you've done this last week I could have done better myself in half an hour. Drat the woodsmoke! It gets in a body's eyes till they can't see a thing." And she hobbled into the hut, working her mouth sourly and rubbing her eyes with the back of her hand.

Nerryn ran into the forest, going cornerways up the mountain, so as not to pass too close to the mill where old Timorash lay sleeping in the sun.

Soon she had to slow down because the way was so steep. And the grass grew thicker and thicker, hairy, sticky, all twined and matted together, as high as her waist. Presently, as she hacked and cut at it with her bone knife, she heard a harsh croaking and flapping above her. She looked up, and saw two grey vultures perched on a branch, leaning forward to peer down at her. Their wings were twice the length of a man's arm and they had long, wrinkled, black, leathery necks and little fierce yellow eyes. As she stood, two more, then five, ten, twenty others came rousting through the branches, and all perched round about, craning down their long black necks, swaying back and forth, keeping balanced by the way they opened and shut their wings.

Nerryn felt very much afraid of them, but she unslung the harp from her back and began to play a soft, trickling tune, like rain falling on a deep pool. Very soon the vultures sank their necks down between their shoulders and closed their eyes. They sat perfectly still.

When she was certain they were asleep, Nerryn made haste to cut and slash at the grass. She was several hundred yards on her way before the vultures woke and came cawing and jostling through the branches to cluster again just over-head. Quickly she pulled the harp round and strummed on its fishbone strings until once again, lulled by the music, the vultures sank their heads between their grey wings and slept. Then she went back to cutting the grass, as fast as she could.

It was a long, tiring way. Soon she grew so weary that she could hardly push one foot ahead of the other, and it was hard to keep awake; once she only just roused in time when a vulture, swooping down, missed her with his beak and instead struck the harp on her back with a loud strange twang that set echoes scampering through the trees.

At last the forest began to thin and dwindle; here the tree-trunks and branches were all draped about with grey-green moss, like long dangling hanks of sheepswool. Moss grew on the rocky ground, too, in a thick carpet. When she reached this part, Nerryn could go on safely; the vultures rose in an angry flock and flew back with harsh croaks of disappoint-ment, for they feared the trailing moss would wind round their wings and trap them.

As soon as she reached the edge of the trees Nerryn lay down in a deep tussock of moss and fell fast asleep.

She was so tired that she slept almost till nightfall, but then the cold woke her. It was bitter on the bare mountainside; the ground was all crisp with white frost, and when Nerryn started walking uphill she crunched through it, leaving deep black footprints. Unless she kept moving she knew that she would probably die of cold, so she climbed on, higher and higher; the stars came out, showing more frost-covered slopes ahead and all round, while the forest far below curled round the flank of the mountain like black fur.

Through the night she went on climbing and by sunrise she had reached the foot of a steep slope of ice-covered boulders. When she tried to climb over these she only slipped back again.

What shall I do now? Nerryn wondered. She stood blowing on her frozen fingers and thought, "I must go on or I shall die here of cold. I will play a tune on the harp to warm my fingers and my wits."

She unslung the harp. It was hard to play, for her fingers were almost numb and at first refused to obey but, while she had climbed the hill, a very sweet, lively tune had come into her head, and she struggled and struggled until her stubborn fingers found the right notes to play it. Once she played the tune — twice — and the stones on the slope above began to roll and shift. She played a third time and, with a thunderous roar, the whole pile broke loose and went sliding down the mountain-side. Nerryn was only just able to dart aside out of the way before the frozen mass careered past, sending up a smoking dust of ice.

Trembling a little, she went on up the hill, and now she

came to a gate in a great wall, set about with towers. The gate stood open, and so she walked through.

"Surely this must be my father's city," she thought.

But when she stood inside the gate, her heart sank, and she remembered old Saroon's words. For the city that must once have been bright with gold and coloured stone and gay with music was all silent; not a soul walked the streets and the houses, under their thick covering of frost, were burnt and blackened by fire.

And, what was still more frightening, when Nerryn looked through the doorways into the houses, she could see people standing or sitting or lying, frozen still like statues, as the cold had caught them while they worked, or slept, or sat at dinner.

"Where shall I go now?" she thought. "It would have been better to stay with Saroon in the forest. When night comes I shall only freeze to death in this place."

But still she went on, almost tiptoeing in the frosty silence of the city, looking into doorways and through gates, until she came to a building that was larger than any other, built with a high roof and many pillars of white marble. The fire had not touched it.

"This must be the temple," she thought, remembering the tale Saroon had told, and she walked between the pillars, which glittered like white candles in the light from the rising sun. Inside there was a vast hall, and many people standing frozen, just as they had been when they came to pray for deliverance from their trouble. They had offerings with them, honey and cakes and white doves and lambs and precious ointment. At the back of the hall the people wore rough clothes of homespun cloth, but farther forward Nerryn saw wonderful robes, embroidered with gold and copper thread, made of rich materials, trimmed with fur and sparkling stones. And up in the very front, kneeling on the steps of the altar, was a man who was finer than all the rest and Nerryn thought he must have been the king himself. His hair and long beard were white, his cloak was purple, and on his head were three crowns, one gold, one copper, and one of ivory. Nerryn stole up to him and touched the fingers that held a gold staff, but they were ice-cold and still as marble, like all the rest.

A sadness came over her as she looked at the people and she thought, "What use to them are their fine robes now? Why did the goddess punish them? What did they do wrong?"

But there was no answer to her question.

"I had better leave this place before I am frozen as well," she thought. "The goddess may be angry with me too, for coming here. But first I will play for her on my harp, as I have not brought any offering."

So she took her harp and began to play. She played all the tunes she could remember, and last of all she played the one that had come into her head as she climbed the mountain.

At the noise of her playing, frost began to fall in white showers from the roof of the temple, and from the rafters and pillars and the clothes of the motionless people. Then the king sneezed. Then there was a stirring noise, like the sound of a winter stream when the ice begins to melt. Then someone laughed aloud, clear laugh. And, just as, outside the town, the pile of frozen rocks had started to move and topple when Nerryn played, so now the whole gathering of people began to stretch themselves, and turn round, and look at one another, and smile. And as she went on playing they began to dance.

The dancing spread, out of the temple and down the streets. People in the houses stood up and danced. Still dancing, they fetched brooms and swept away the heaps of frost that kept falling from the rooftops with the sound of the music. They fetched old wooden pipes and tabors out of cellars that had escaped the fire, so that when Nerryn stopped playing at last, quite tired out, the music still went on. All day and all night, for thirty days, the music lasted, until the houses were rebuilt, the streets clean, and not a speck of frost remained in the city.

But the king beckoned Nerryn aside when she stopped playing and they sat down on the steps of the temple.

"My child," he said, "where did you get that harp?"

"Sir, I made it out of fishbones after a picture of my father's harp that an old woman made for me."

"And what was your father's name, child, and where is he now?"

"Sir, he is dead in the forest, but here is a piece of a tablet with his name on it." And Nerryn held out the little fragment with Heramon the harper's name written. When he saw it, great tears formed in the king's eyes and began to roll down his cheeks.

"Sir," Nerryn said, "what is the matter? Why do you weep?"

"I weep for my son Heramon, who is lost, and I weep for joy because my grandchild has returned to me."

Then the king embraced Nerryn and took her to his palace and had robes of fur and velvet put on her, and there was great happiness and much feasting. And the king told

Nerryn how, many years ago, the goddess was angered because the people had grown so greedy for gold from her mountain that they spent their lives in digging and mining, day and night, and forgot to honour her with music, in her temple and in the streets, as they had been used to do. They made tools of gold, and plates and dishes and musical instruments; everything that could be was made of gold. So at last the goddess appeared among them, terrible with rage, and put a curse on them, of burning and freezing.

"Since you prefer gold, got by burrowing in the earth, to the music that should honour me," she said, "you may keep your golden toys and little good may they do you! Let your golden harps and trumpets be silent, your flutes and pipes be dumb! I shall not come among you again until I am summoned by notes from a harp that is not made of gold, nor of silver, nor any precious metal, a harp that has never touched the earth but came from deep water, a harp that no man has ever played."

Then fire burst out of the mountain, destroying houses and killing many people. The king ordered his son Heramon, who was the bravest man in the city, to cross the dangerous forest and seek far and wide until he should find the harp of which the goddess spoke. Before Heramon could depart a great cold had struck, freezing people where they stood; only just in time he caught up his little daughter from her cradle and carried her away with him.

"But now you are come back," the old king said, "you shall be queen after me, and we shall take care that the goddess is honoured with music every day, in the temple and in the streets. And we will order everything that is made of gold to be thrown into the mountain torrent, so that nobody ever again shall be tempted to worship gold before the goddess."

So this was done, the king himself being the first to throw away his golden crown and staff. The river carried all the golden things down through the forest until they came to rest in Timorash's millpool, and one day, when he was fishing for carp, he pulled out the crown. Overjoyed, he ground it to powder and sold it to his neighbours for barley wine. Then he returned to the pool, hoping for more gold, but by now he was so drunk that he fell in and was drowned among a clutter of golden spades and trumpets and goblets and pickaxes.

But long before this Nerryn, with her harp on her back and astride of a white mule with knives bound to its hoofs, had ridden down the mountain to fetch Saroon as she had promised. She passed the forest safely, playing music for the vultures while the mule cut its way through the long grass. Nobody in the village recognized her, so splendidly was she dressed in fur and scarlet.

But when she came to where Saroon's hut had stood, the ground was bare, nor was there any trace that a dwelling had ever been there. And when she asked for Saroon, nobody knew the name, and the whole village declared that such a person had never been there.

Amazed and sorrowful, Nerryn returned to her grandfather. But one day, not long after, when she was alone, praying in the temple of the goddess, she heard a voice that said,

"Sing, child!"

And Nerryn was greatly astonished, for she felt she had heard the voice before, though she could not think where. While she looked about her, wondering, the voice said again,

"Sing!"

And then Nerryn understood, and she laughed, and, taking her harp, sang a song about chopping wood, and about digging, and fishing, and the birds of the forest, and how the stream's voice changes in summer and in winter. For now she knew who had helped her to make her harp of fish-bones.

A Small Pinch of Weather

———•———

Petronilla's Guesthouse, where the bishop stayed, was next door to a little shop with small and unimpressive windows containing a mixed-up tangle of things which nobody ever looked at, because they always walked straight into the shop and told Miss Sophy Ross what they wanted, and she always had it, whether it was three ounces of three-ply for a jersey or half a mile of mare's-tail for Tuesday.

The previous woolmonger before Miss Sophy had been an old lady who had called the shop Joy. The signboard read like this:

WOOLS AND JOY EMBROIDERY

with the "Joy" in bigger letters to show it was intended to be read first. Of course nobody ever did. They called the shop *Wools and Joy*. When the old lady died, Sophy's father gave her the shop for a twenty-first birthday present and suggested she should change the name to "Wools and Sophy", but she preferred to call it *Wools and Weather Embroidery*, and had the sign changed accordingly.

The town of Strathcloud, where the Ross family lived, still employed an official weather witch. The post was hereditary. So at twenty-one Sophy had automatically become Weather Operator for the Strathcloud Urban District Council at a salary of four pounds a year, a bushel of sunflower seeds, and free upkeep of her bicycle.

Her duties were simple: she had to provide suitable weather for any town occasion, such as bonfire night, or the ceremonial ducking-of-the-provost, which took place on April 1. And when these fixtures were dealt with she was free to make weather bookings for any private citizens who wanted them, provided they did not conflict.

"Half an hour's rain for your carrots, Mr McCrae, Tuesday morning? I'm afraid eleven-thirty to twelve is booked sunny for Mrs Lowrie — Janet Lowrie's wedding, you know; would twelve to twelve-thirty suit? Fine rain, or medium fine? And do you want any wind with it?"

There was no charge for the weather itself, but a sixpenny booking fee which went toward municipal expenses.

When the Bishop of Mbutambuta retired from Africa and came to live in Strathcloud he stayed at Petronilla's Guesthouse. On his first day exploring the town he was attracted by the *Wools and Weather Embroidery* notice. He wandered into the shop and stared around at the crochet hooks, dangling skeins of wool, needle measures, rain gauges, and wind scales.

"Guid morning," said Miss Sophy, "what can I do for you?"

It was impossible to tell Miss Sophy's age. She had not

changed since she took office at twenty-one. She was small, her face was nut-shaped and nut-brown, her hair was mousy, and her eyes were gray. There was something a little vague and misty about her, but she had a nice smile.

"Oh, I'd like a hemstitched sunset, please," said the bishop absently, looking at Miss Sophy, "and half a pound of three-ply hail."

The bishop and Miss Sophy became good friends for a short time. The bishop had been acquainted with rainmakers in Mbutambuta, and was interested to find the old custom kept up in Scotland.

"Where does your weather end?" he asked. "Does it extend to Farquhidder?"

"Oh no, that would never do!" said Miss Sophy, shocked. "The weather stops at the parish boundary, of course. Sometimes in a drought we get people standing there with buckets and hoses trying to siphon off our rain."

"Why don't they make their own rain?"

"Oh well, they've never had a weather witch in Farquhidder."

Miss Sophy was very fond of every kind of weather. When her duties permitted, she liked to go in the rain or the mist or the sun, riding her bicycle over the moors and watching the clouds whirl across the sky or the raindrops slide off the end of her handle bars. The bishop was a great walker, and sometimes she would see him, always equipped with his umbrella, striding up the local mountain or down one of its glens.

But alas, Miss Sophy had very little spare time. That was one of the penalties of the job: she had to be always within reach or near at hand in case of emergency calls on her services.

The trouble between Miss Sophy and the bishop was due to Sophy's sunshine-colored cat, Tomintoul.

The bishop slept up on the top story of Petronilla's Guesthouse, in a large spacious room with a picture window and a skylight.

Recently Tomintoul had taken to roaming at night. Perhaps he found Miss Sophy's diet insufficient for his large frame — she lived mostly on fried eggs, done sunny side up, apple snow, and sunshine cake with ice-cream frosting. Whether Tomintoul hoped for better things at the guesthouse, or whether he had personal affairs farther afield, who can say? At all events, he went out several times a week, and the route he took was over the roof and through the room occupied by the bishop, who was quite unused to having a large, dew-spangled cat descend on him heavily in the middle of the night. The first time it happened he thought Tomintoul was a python (they had been the chief nuisance in Mbutambuta), and leaped yelling across the room. The second time he didn't wake up, but as Tomintoul, finding the door shut, spread his large form across more and more of the bed, the bishop began to suffer from strange dreams. He thought he was being hugged by bears, run over by steam rollers, drowned in a river full of crocodiles.

Next morning found Tomintoul placidly washing in the middle of the bed while its rightful owner dangled in a fold of blanket at one side.

The bishop felt he was being treated with lack of respect, and complained to Miss Dalziel, who ran the guesthouse.

"Och, awa' could ye not keep the skylight shut?" she suggested.

"That is out of the question," said the bishop firmly. "It

was in order to benefit from the crisp, healthy air that I came to Scotland. If this persecution continues I doubt if it will be possible for me to make a prolonged stay at your otherwise delightful guesthouse, where I had hoped to spend my declining days."

"Well, noo, we could find you anither room."

"But I like the outlook from this one. All that is needful is that the cat be shut in at night."

But when Miss Sophy heard this suggestion she exclaimed, "Shut in Tomintoul? Impossible! Besides, I need to study the condition of his fur in the morning. It tells me a lot about the weather."

Unfortunately, Tomintoul's wanderings became more and more frequent. Next night he arrived on the bishop at 2 AM with a large mouse, alighting so heavily that the bishop, who was dreaming that he was aboard the Titanic, shouted, "Abandon ship! Man the lifeboats!"

No bishop likes to feel ridiculous. Next morning he determined to curse Tomintoul with bell, book, and candle. As it happened, however, the ship on which he had traveled from the Gold Coast had been overrun by mice, and his stock of cursing candles had been consumed at lively mouse parties. The bishop entered MacGregor's Stores at nine o'clock next morning and asked for a pound of their largest candles.

"I'm afraid we're clean out of candles," said Miss Maggie MacGregor. "Can I sell you a nice wee electric torch, now?"

"Oh, leave it, leave it," the bishop said wearily. In mitigation of his irritability it must be remembered that he was low on sleep.

Miss Sophy was dreamily stacking pink, blue, and green wools into a rainbow-colored pyramid and gazing at the weather outside (a nice drizzle, lightly touched with sleet) when the bishop stormed in.

"This must stop!" he said accusingly.

"Only another ten minutes," said Sophy comfortably," "and then we're due for a rainbow to coincide with the children's break. Don't you like rain? Can I sell you some wool? Many retired clerical gentlemen take to knitting."

And before he knew where he was the bishop had bought eighteen ounces of fishermen's knit and two immense wooden needles.

He took the bus to Farquhidder to buy a catapult and a quantity of netting, and a potato pistol, and a fire extinguisher.

After he had made these purchases he dropped into a cafe for a cup of tea, and there chanced to overhear a very odd conversation.

"Going to the races, Thursday?" a weaselly-looking little man was saying to another who was rather like a tall guinea pig, hairless, with pink eyes.

"Why, got any good tips?"

"I've one very good tip." Weasel leaned closer and looked sharply about. "You remember MacPhairos's Marsh Marigold? The mare that only runs well when the going's sticky?"

"I thought he'd given up running her."

"Man, he's had a stroke of genius. Ye ken Strathcloud, where they have the lass that sees to the weather?"

"She's never going to — "

"Hush, man! Listen to this!" Weasel leaned closer, and the bishop heard the words "rowan . . . soon settle her."

He thought to himself that if Marsh Marigold's winning the race depended on someone trying to bribe Miss Sophy, then the horse's backers were out of luck. For though he would gladly have transported her and her cat to the farthest Antipodes, the bishop was quite sure Miss Sophy would never be party to such a plan.

When Tomintoul came to call on the bishop very early next morning he received a rude shock. Jumping down through the skylight he found himself entangled in innumerable folds of strawberry netting, and the bishop bombarded him with potato pellets and sprayed him with detergent foam. Tomintoul was affronted.

"And you can stay there till after breakfast to teach you the sanctity of the English home," the bishop said crossly, and went down to his porridge, leaving Tomintoul in a sadly ruffled condition, sniffing the heartbreaking fragrance of kippers that wafted up the stairs.

After breakfast the bishop went for a short stroll, according to custom. But the weaver was inclement (in fact it was raining cats and dogs) and he soon turned homeward. As he neared the guesthouse he noticed an anxious crowd gathered outside the woolshop next door.

Miss Dalziel was there, and Mr McRae, and Mrs Lowrie, and Miss Maggie MacGregor, and a great many other people, some inside the shop and some on the step, all looking worried and distressed.

"Oh, Bishop dear!" Miss Dalziel burst out as soon as he came within earshot. "You'll not have seen Miss Sophy the morn? It's not like her to leave the shop, but no one's laid eyes on her since eight o'clock!"

"No, I haven't seen her," said the bishop. Then he remembered Tomintoul, still incarcerated upstairs. Would the cat's imprisonment have anything to do with Miss Sophy's

absence? Hurriedly excusing himself, he went up to his bedroom, where Tomintoul, making the best of a bad job, had
curled up and gone to sleep.

"Wake up," said the bishop, "your mistress is missing."
He loosed Tomintoul from the nets, and took him down to
the shop. By this time the police had arrived and were
searching for clues, but not finding any.

"We'll need to be telling the provost of this," said Inspector Trootie. "But he's awa' doon at tile races all day today."

The races! Only then did the bishop remember the ominous conversation he had overheard in the cafe at Farquhidder. He told Inspector Trootie about it.

"Man! Then it's as plain as can be! Yon miscreants will
have kidnaped her and be forcing her to make a bit of rain
for them."

"Och, maircy, the puir lassie," lamented Miss Dalziel.
"Whatever shall we do for weather without her? Saints pre-
sairve us, it'll never stop raining!"

But just at that moment the rain did stop in a sudden and
most decisive manner. The sun came out and shone as if it
intended to go on shining all night.

"Good for the lassie, she's defying the scoondrels,"
exclaimed Inspector Trootie. "I wonder, noo, where they'll
have taken her? We'll be needing police dogs to follow the
scent, and the mischance of it is they're all in Hyde Park, taking part in the sheep-dog trials."

"Could we no' put Tomintoul on the trail?" suggested
Miss Dalziel.

Ah, it's easy to see ye've a hand in the administrative side
of things, ma'am," said Inspector Trootie admiringly.

Tomintoul had vanished again. After some searching he

was discovered back in Petronilla's Guesthouse, availing himself of the kipper skins. He was brought back licking his whiskers and put on to the scent at the woolshop door, though, as the inspector observed, "if he can deduce ony-thing through yon reek of kipper he's better than a marvel."

The weather was behaving very oddly. In a series of short spells they had fog, sleet, snow, wind that shot up from gale force seven to twelve and then back to six; rainbows, snow-bows, blistering sun, and a very muddling series of mirages due to the constant variation in air temperature.

"I doot they're subjecting her to pressure," Inspector Trootie said unhappily.

Tomintoul was a very slow tracker. He kept sitting down to wash, and this was maddening for the pursuers.

Old McCrae said dourly, "I've heard tell of tracking doon wrongdoers with a posse, but aiblins this is the first time it's ever been pairpitrated with a pussy."

Tomintoul stuck his right hind leg over his head and looked inscrutably under it at Mr McCrae.

The bishop couldn't bear the pace. He had been used to striding through the bush at a smart four miles an hour, and he soon decided to strike off on his own. Besides, he hadn't much faith in Tomintoul's judgment, and he had been vis-ited by another idea. He climbed the side of Glasdeir, the local mountain, until he reached the bottom end of a lonely glen with a single rowan tree in it.

Meanwhile Tomintoul had dismayed the trackers by returning to Petronilla's Guesthouse and asking in an em-phatic manner for more kipper skins. The inspector thought it would be best if his request was granted, so they all stood around impatiently while he ate two or three. Then he picked up one very large skin and carried it slowly through the village.

"And whut do ye suppose will be the meaning of that?" said Inspector Trootie.

"Hoots, man, can ye not see the guid-hearted cattie is taking a wee bit fush to his mistress in distress?"

"We shan't reach her till Hogmanay at this rate," the inspector said gloomily. "Do ye suppose Tomintoul would let me carry the fush?"

But Tomintoul scorned any such suggestion, and went on sit-down strike, growling loudly every time the inspector tried to approach him. Matters had to be left as they were. The procession wound at a snail's pace down to the bridge over the Hirple Burn and up the hill on the other side toward Mudie's Barn.

At about this time the bishop, approaching his rowan tree along the craggy and twisting glen, heard a series of angry shouts and a faint cry for help. Nodding grimly to himself he rounded the last corner of rock and beheld a strange scene.

Four or five louts, (if he had been Inspector Trootie he would have known they were the "Wild Wee Lads," alias the Ardnafechtan Gang) including the weaselly man from the cafe, had the poor little weather witch tied up in the high fork of the rowan tree, where she looked most uncomfortable. Two of them carried axes, and a couple more were piling dried bracken and whin around the bole of the tree.

"Now for the last and lucky time, lass, will you obleege us with a bit rain?" snarled Hughie Hogg, the weaselly man. "We'd hate to cause you unnecessary suffering, but it's airgently needful for oor plans that the ground should be soaked by three o'clock. If ye will not grant this reasonable request we'll be forced to chop through half the tree and set fire to it."

"I can't let you have any rain," Miss Sophy answered resolutely. "In the first place, you are not Strathcloud rate-payers, and in the second, this afternoon's booked fine to dry the Strathcloud Wanderers' football wash."

"Give her a taste of smoke, Donald," said Hughie. "If we warm her up enough she'll likely make a bit of rain to dowse the fire."

Donald lit a patch of furze, and the smoke puffed up into poor Sophy's face. At the same moment Hughie swung his ax with an ominous clunk against the tree. But the sky remained obstinately blue and cloudless, the sun shone indefatigably.

"You'll have terrible bad luck if you chop a rowan tree," the weather witch said faintly. Then her head drooped sideways and she slipped down in the cords that held her. It was plain that she was unconscious.

"She'll come to soon enough when the fire burns up under her toes," said Donald callously.

"Get her down at once, you abominable blackguards!" snapped the bishop, waving his umbrella.

The gang spun around in amazement. In their absorption they had not noticed him coming. But when they realized they had only an elderly clerical gentleman to deal with, they relaxed and began to close in on him menacingly.

"Ye'll be sorry you came up here, daddy-o," said Hughie.

"Are you going to get that lady down or not?"

"Are ye oot of your mind, man? After all the trouble we've taken to put her there?"

"Then I shall be obliged to shout," said the bishop, putting his hands over his ears.

"Shout and be dommed to ye. There's no one nearer than Strathcloud," said Donald, who had run up and reconnoitered from the shoulder of the glen.

The bishop's shout was a most unusual sound. It had an electrifying effect on the gang. Without a single exception they dropped to the ground as if they had been pole-axed, and lay motionless.

"Miss Sophy!" called the bishop. "Are you all right?"

But it was plain that she was still unconscious, and unfortunately the pile of dried furze beneath her was now blazing merrily.

The bishop took out of his pocket a neatly woven grass string, from which dangled a small cluster of bones. He addressed these in a stern, commanding voice: "Rain, if you please. And make haste."

Gray clouds came scurrying across the sky like poultry running to be fed, and unloosed their contents in a torrential downpour directly over the spot where the bishop stood. He hastily opened his umbrella.

In less than no time the bonfire was quenched and the bishop was able to climb the rowan and rescue Miss Sophy, who was recovering under the reviving effect of a nice drop of rain.

"Oh," she sighed, "how delicious." Then rousing a little more she remembered the situation and exclaimed, "Oh, but this will never do! There was no rain scheduled for this afternoon!"

"Don't be alarmed," said the bishop, "this storm is extremely local." He took off his hat and addressed the teeming heavens. "You may now stop. I am much obliged to you."

"Good gracious," said Miss Sophy weakly, "who taught you to do that?"

"Oh, I learned it from a man in Mbutambuta," the bishop said modestly.

"But how did you dispose of the gang?"

"I used a battle shout which was taught me by the same man. It is most efficacious — in fact it has a literally stunning effect. N'Doko was able to kill people with it, but luckily I am not so proficient. However, those men should stay unconscious long enough for the police to get here."

He picked up Miss Sophy and carried her carefully down the glen.

Where, meanwhile, were the police?

With the rest of the townspeople of Strathcloud they were in Mudie's Barn, indignantly surveying the object of Tomintoul's pilgrimage, a lissom black mother cat and three fine kittens. Tomintoul, intensely proud at all this public notice, gave his wife the kipper skin and set about washing his children.

"The auld wretch! He desairves to be jailed for contempt — leading us a wild-goose chase like this!" cried Miss Dalziel indignantly.

Inspector Trootie was more philosophical. "Aweel, aweel, hoo was he tae ken whit we were seeking? We'll juist have ti goe on sairching for the puir wee leddy."

"But where?" wailed Miss Maggie MacGregor.

Her question was soon answered, for they met the bishop and Miss Sophy by the bridge.

The bishop never told the police how he had managed to

subdue the Ardnafechtan Gang, and they themselves had no theories about it. But they never tried to interfere with the weather witch of Strathcloud again.

From that day the bishop and Miss Sophy were firm friends again. Tomintoul's family was brought down to the woolshop (where it wrought terrible havoc, but nobody minded) so he had no need to go out over rooftops at night to visit them.

In due course the black kitten went to live with the bishop, who christened it Kattegat, and it was an interesting fact that, although Kattegat slept on the bishop's bed, taking up more and more room as he grew larger and larger, the bishop never again threatened to leave Petronilla's Guest-house. Indeed, he soon fell into the habit of giving Miss Sophy a hand with the weather, if she was ever a bit under it, or wanted a day off to go blaeberry picking.

The bishop never achieved Sophy's lightness of touch with the elements, though; and when the sun shone hot enough to fry an egg, or the wind shot up to Beaufort Scale twelve, or the hailstones were as large as Seville oranges, the good people of Strathcloud would shake their heads and remark,

"Ah, to be sure, yon's a touch o' bishop's weather."

The King Who Stood All Night

It was the evening before the coronation. Although the November day had been cold and blowy, and an icy dust was drifting about the streets of Cuckoo City, people were everywhere. The mayor and corporation were clambering up and down gray walls with yards of bunting, and little boys were swinging across streets on ropes of flags. Men had set up stalls of rattles and streamers, hot meat pies were being sold by the dozen, and street sweepers had abandoned their usual job and were scattering sand across the broad square between the palace and the cathedral.

Cuckoo Land was not very large, and the whole population had come down to the capital for the celebrations. All day they had been streaming down from the mountains, on foot, on horseback, and in carriages, and now the lucky ones were getting ready to go to bed in inns or friends' houses, while the unlucky stood or sat patiently in the streets and parks. The leaves drifted down from the chestnut trees, where cuckoos perched in May, and little boys played conkers and were chased about in the dusk by their anxious parents.

All the population? No, not quite. Far off in the mountains a tearful little boy and his father were loading their donkey with straw hats. They were very poor, and had waited to finish the last few hats before starting, in order to sell them in Cuckoo City while they were there. But the boy was young, and though both had worked hard, the hats had taken longer than they expected; they were very late in setting out, and it was almost dark as they went down the steep hill toward the plain.

"Up on the donkey with you, Paul," said his father. "You must get some sleep tonight, or you'll never stay awake for the fireworks and shows tomorrow evening. I'll lead the donkey — I don't need so much sleep nowadays."

But Paul's eyes refused to stay shut — he was too excited and too worried in case they missed their way in the dark and arrived late. So he walked on the other side of the donkey and held on to the pannier.

"Hurry, Father," he kept saying, "the coronation begins at eight in the morning, remember."

"I can't go any faster than this," grumbled his father, "and nor can Matilda with that great load of hats."

✦   ✦   ✦

Meanwhile in the cathedral, charwomen were still scrubbing and polishing the great tiled floor, huge silk and satin draperies were being hung from galleries, and officials ran about with bits of paper and pencils, still working out where everyone was to stand, who was to come in first, and how the dukes and duchesses were to be given cups of hot tea if they felt faint.

In the palace the cooks had prepared a wonderful banquet and were still icing the cake, while the grooms of the chamber were putting the last touches to the king's robes — flicking minute grains of dust off the ermine, blowing on the crown and polishing it, tweaking the white silk stockings to make sure they would not ladder. Fussily presiding over them was the lord chancellor. Every few minutes he hurried away to give the young king some last words of advice on etiquette, and then the grooms heaved sighs of relief and stopped work for a few minutes, mopping their brows.

The new king had been brought up in the country. He was not used to court life, and was being worn out by the lord chancellor's tiresome advice. When he heard the door open for the fifteenth time he sighed deeply and strolled over to the window. Pushing back the curtains, which had been drawn at least an hour before it was necessary, he looked out into the windy square.

"Just look at all those people!" he exclaimed in surprise. "What can they be doing in the square at this time of day? There won't be anything to see till tomorrow morning."

"Oh, they are the people who haven't been able to get rooms," replied the lord chancellor. "They'll spend the night in the square. But what I was going to say to Your Majesty was that when you greet the ambassadors — "

"But, goodness gracious," interrupted the king, "You don't mean to say that they are going to stand all night in the square? Why, it's freezing — "

"They don't mind," said the lord chancellor, smiling his toothy smile. "They think it's well worth it to have a good view of the royal procession. Now, as I was saying — "

But the young king was deeply troubled.

"If they are going to stand all night in the cold just for the chance of seeing me, I think it would be only right if everyone inside the palace stood all night too. Please send out a message to the court."

"Your Majesty, that would never do!" exclaimed the lord chancellor in horror. "Have the whole court stay awake all night! Think of the effect on foreign royalties and ambassadors. Why, they would be terribly offended. No, no, that would never do."

"Perhaps you are right," replied the king with a sigh. But when the chancellor had given his advice and gone away, the king gave orders that no one else was to be admitted to the royal presence that evening.

"At least I can do something myself," he thought, and he dressed quickly in some plain dark clothes, and went out by an inconspicuous side entrance into the square.

At this time little Paul and his father were making good progress down the mountain path, when suddenly there was a clink of iron on stone, and the donkey began to hobble.

"Oh, Father," cried Paul in despair. "Matilda has cast a shoe. What shall we do?"

"Don't worry," said his father. "We aren't far from Matthew the smith's forge. I expect he'll be gone by now, but he won't mind if we borrow his tools. Pick up any firewood you see as we go along, and we'll soon have a fire to shoe Matilda again."

Soon they reached the forge, and little Paul ran about gathering wood while his father heated the cast shoe in the fire, and Matilda stood patiently waiting. It was not long before the shoe was nailed in position.

They loaded the donkey again, and were just about to

leave the shed, when they heard a loud and terrible roaring on the mountainside. Even Paul's father turned pale. "We shall have to stay inside," he said. "That is a mountain lion."

✦   ✦   ✦

The king strolled across the dusky square to the park railings and leaned against them, shivering a little. There was an old man selling roast chestnuts and hot pies which smelled very tempting. He put his hand in his pocket for money, and then realized that he had come without any — he was so unused to buying things for himself.

The old man saw his wistful look and chuckled.

"Have one on the house, son," he said. "We don't have a coronation every day." And he gave the king a succulent pie and a generous handful of hot chestnuts.

✦   ✦   ✦

Paul and his father huddled together in terror as the mountain lion ranged around the little forge. Only the glow of the fire prevented it from breaking down the flimsy door, and soon their stock of wood would be exhausted.

"We shall never get there in time for the procession now," said little Paul miserably, and his father's thoughts were more gloomy still.

But just at that moment there came the trampling of many horses outside, and the lion slunk off, disappointed.

"Who's in there?" cried a voice, and there came a thunderous knock at the door.

Paul and his father stared at one another. It must be a band of robbers!

✦   ✦   ✦

Meanwhile the king and the old pieman had fallen into con-versation. It was quite dark now and the pieman had covered up his wares with a tarpaulin, thrown a corner of it over his shoulders to keep out the frost, and lit his pipe.

"They say he's a fine young king," he said. "I remember his dad's coronation, and his grandad's before him. He was a fine old man too. Easy and pleasant as you please, but he never let anyone bamboozle him or disobey him. They say he had all the lords and dukes and princes too, running around as scared as a lot of schoolboys."

The young king sighed, thinking of the lord chancellor. "I wish I was like that," he said, half to himself.

"Ah, you're young yet," said the old man. "But you'll learn. I don't know what trade you're in, but you'll find peo-ple anywhere are like sheep. When I was a young lad I was a shepherd, and the first time I was out with the sheep I could have sat down and cried. However many times I ran around and around the flock, I couldn't fetch them through the gate into the fold. I was getting flustered and fidgety, so I sat down and scratched my head. 'Paul,' I said to myself, 'you're a fool,' and I picked up the old bellwether, the head of the flock, and dumped her through the gate. All the rest of them followed through, easy as pie. People are just the same — once the most important one's through the gate, you've got 'em all. You just have to know your mind." He sniffed the air. "Bitter tonight. Reminds me of the old days on the moun-tain. You'd better have a corner of this over you, lad." And he threw another corner of waterproof sheet over the king's shoulders. Midnight was striking.

✦   ✦   ✦

When Paul's father opened the smithy door he found that the men were not robbers after all, but a band of guards patrolling the kingdom to make sure that all was well while people were away from their homes.

"We'll give you a convoy down to the plain," said the leader. "You men, take them on your horses, and George, lead the donkey."

So they went clattering down the gorge with laughter and shouting, under the paling dawn sky.

"We part here," said the leader. "Think of us at the celebrations. Here's something for your breakfast." He gave them a great sausage.

Matilda was loosed, and they set off again, turning now and then to wave to the kindly soldiers.

"How far is it to the city?" asked Paul.

"Twenty miles," said his father, sighing. "I'm afraid we won't be there till midday now. Your grandfather will be worrying about us."

Little Paul said nothing, but as he walked manfully forward, two large tears rolled down his dusty cheeks.

✦   ✦   ✦

As the day became brighter over the palace square, the crowd began to yawn and stretch. People brought out food and had breakfast. The old pieman, who had been telling stories about his mountain days, unpacked his wares once more, and relit his brazier, helped by the king. He looked keenly about the square.

"I'm expecting my son and grandson," he said. "They were coming down from the mountains last night. They should be here by now." He began to tell the king about the straw hat business, and how they varied the shapes to suit the customers.

As the hands of the clock moved toward eight the crowd began to crane and peer expectantly toward the palace gates. The king, too, gazed in the direction toward which all heads were turned.

"What are they looking for?" he asked.

"Have you forgotten it's coronation day?" the pieman said. "Any minute now the king will be coming out in his golden coach. Why, what's the matter, lad?" For the young man had turned toward him a face of blank dismay.

"Why, that's me! I'd forgotten all about it!" he exclaimed, and without another word he began running toward the palace, dodging and twisting through the crowd, and leaving the old man open-mouthed.

There was a scene of terrible confusion in the palace, as courtiers searched here and there for the king. When he arrived, puffing and panting, the lord chancellor turned on him reproachfully.

"Your Majesty! The grooms have been waiting for three hours to dress you. The whole ceremony will have to be postponed till twelve. We shall never get you robed before then."

The king looked at him miserably. All those poor people in the square would now have to wait nearly four hours more, and it was beginning to rain. And this was all his fault.

A sudden idea came to him. "Very well," he said. "If it will take another three hours to dress me — though it seems ridiculous — we must invite all the poor people to come in and have a nap in the palace."

The Chancellor looked as if he would burst. "All those common people? Impossible!"

"I mean it," said the king, coldly. "Hurry up and have it proclaimed. They can sleep on the carpets, as there won't be enough beds. And tea will be served."

The chancellor looked at the king and suddenly collapsed. "Very well, Your Majesty," he said meekly, and left to give the order. Soon people began streaming into the palace and settling gratefully to sleep in the great warm rooms, on thick, soft carpets.

The grooms of the chamber began to work on the king, slowly and carefully. But as they put on the silk stockings, his head nodded, and by the time he had been draped in the great velvet cloak, he was fast asleep.

✦   ✦   ✦

When little Paul and his father arrived in the palace square, there was not a soul in sight. The great space lay perfectly silent.

Paul, who had kept up very bravely till then, began to cry. "It's all over," he sobbed. "Oh, I did hope there'd be some of the carriages and flags still about. Now I'll never know what it was like."

"We'd better go to Grandfather's house," said his father sadly. "He'll be wondering what's happened to us."

But as they spoke, and were about to turn away, the old pie seller came hurrying across the square from the palace.

"I've been watching for you," he said cheerfully. "Coronation's been put off because the king's fast asleep, poor young lad, and no one could wake him. We're all having a bit of a lie-down in the palace, and what do you think — the king's invited you and me and little Paul here to have supper with him tonight."

All afternoon the tired-out people slept on the soft palace carpets. Little Paul and his father slept among them, and in the evening they had supper with the king in his private apartments.

Next day the coronation took place — and what a day that was!

Cat's Cradle

———◆———

There were two Shugger sisters, Minnie and Wendy; Minnie, the elder, was fat and loving and a good cook besides; her *Turnip Delight* was something you'd remember to your dying day, and her *Parsley Crumble* and *Raspberry Frushie* won first prize every summer at the Flatsea Church Fete; everybody was fond of Minnie, and everybody grieved when she died, untimely, at age twenty, of the measles complicated by an inflammation she'd caught picking gooseberries in the pouring rain to make jam for a sailor friend of hers. Wendy, just the opposite of her sister, was thin, pretty, and spiteful; she had a tongue that could have been hired out by the hour for wood-sanding and paint-stripping jobs; it'd take the hide off a dromedary. And she had a dog to match; have you noticed how often people's dogs are like an offshoot of their own selves, the dog doing all the things its owner would like to but doesn't dare? This dog, Jobbie his name was, barked daylong and nightlong; his thin peevish yap could be heard from end to end of the village; and he chased kids and bit the postman and tore holes in people's fences and garden beds and carpets, and worried cats when he could catch them and stole any food he could grab. He was a big brown poodle, as big as a pig.

"What a shame it was Minnie had to die," a lot of people said. "Why couldn't it have been th'other one? *She'd* have been spared easy enough — she and that big ugly monster of hers."

Of course, overhearing remarks like that turned Wendy no sweeter; and it was surprising how many she did overhear. Many were the black looks she gave and received. No one in the village liked her, and not a man would offer for her, in spite of her pretty face and her father's soap factory.

Well, when young Martin Keystone came home from sea one time, off his ship the *Escallonia*, who should be there to greet him, all smiles on the dockside, but Wendy Shugger, with her big clumsy dog behind her.

"Martin! My love!" cries out Wendy, in a voice like treacle and vinegar mixed together, and she flings her skinny arms around Martin's neck in a throttling grip, and the dog, Jobbie, right alongside, bobbing about like a thirty-pound earwig, anxious to be in on anything that was taking place.

"Pleased to see you, I'm sure, Miss Wendy!" gasped Martin, very startled, his eyes roaming about over her shoulder among the crowd as he tried to wrestle himself out of her embrace without being too conspicuous about it. "But where's Miss Minnie? Where's your sister? Is she any-where about?"

"Oh, she's dead," said Wendy carelessly. "Dead and buried these four months. But *I'm* alive, Martin my love, and so happy that you want to marry me, and I've got a special

licence, which Pa procured as soon as your ship was sighted off the Dodman, and the Reverend Grope is all a-readied to marry us on Saturday, for I knew you'd not want to wait a minute more than you need, Martin dear, once you'd set foot on shore!"

"Wh-wh-what?" stammered Martin, his jaw dropping right down and his face going as white as a sail that's new out of the bo'sun's locker. "What did you say, miss?"

"I was so happy, Martin, when I got your letter from Valparaiso asking me to marry you," said Wendy, looking at him out of the corners of her eyes. "That letter filled me with such overflowing joy that I've carried it round with me ever since. I couldn't abear to let it out of my sight. Nights it's been under my pillow, days I've had it tucked into my cuff!"

And she fetched out a gray-looking dog-eared envelope addressed in Martin's handwriting to "Miss W. Shugger."

"But — " began Martin faintly.

"When Minnie was alive," Wendy went on with a smile so sweet you could have preserved crab apples in it, "when Minnie was alive — being as her name was really Wilhelmina, as you know, Martin — there sometimes used to be complications about which of the letters that came to the house was meant for her, and which was meant for me — both our names beginning with a *W* made it awkward. But of course, as Minnie was the older, she should have been addressed as 'Miss Shugger,' and any letters for 'Miss W. Shugger' was properly mine. But, anyway, Martin, when your dear letter came, I knew it must be meant for me, because of the sweet thing you said in it, for well I remember how much you enjoyed my apple tart that time when you came to our house for tea just before you went off to sea!"

Poor Martin, with a shudder, remembered how after

Minnie's delicious *Parsley Crumble* he'd been obliged to eat a piece of Wendy's apple tart, which was like a layer of beaverboard with a little sour green paste atop of it; he had done his best to be polite about it as he forced down a few mouthfuls.

"Oh, what a beautiful letter that was!" sighed Wendy, pulling the paper out from its envelope, and gazing at it rapturously, she read it aloud: "Dear Miss Shugger, will you be mine? A girl what can cook like you deserves to live in a palace, but just the same I hope you will share the humble home my Gran has left me at number two, The Saltings, when I get home from this trip, for Captain Egg has promised me mate's berth next time out, and Granny Keystone has also left me £200 in the post office. Your devoted admirer, Martin." Oh, Martin my love, was ever a proposal more beautifully worded?"

"I — I don't know, I'm sure," says Martin, shivering as if he had the quinsy. "The thing is, you see, Miss — "

"And Ma and Pa are so happy about it," went on Wendy, "and so are all my aunts and uncles. Ma and Pa couldn't wait to congratulate us — here they are."

Mr and Mrs Shugger were like two underdone cottage loaves, fat and white and squat; they came trotting along all wreathed in smiles, and their little beady eyes were sparkling bright as new sixpences, and Mr Shugger worked Martin's hand up and down as if he were trying to force water from a rusty pump. "You and me's going to get on fine, young man, I know that," he kept saying. "Ah, you're one as keeps your word and does your bit, I know; there's some as makes promises and then sheers off again, but you're not one of that kind, I'll wager my soap amalgamator; and just as well, too, for if you was to sheer off and leave my Wendy in the lurch, I'd clap an action for breach of promise on you so fast you'd wish your ship had gone to to the bottom in the South Atlantic. But we won't talk about disagreeable subjects," he says, "for I know you are pure sterling, young Martin, and will stand by my daughter through thick and thin, and through thick most particular. In fact," he says, "since we all have such an esteem for you, Martin, my dear boy, I shouldn't wonder but what I and my dear wife might come along to live with you as well, at number two, The Saltings, for to keep Wendy company when you are off at sea; the poor girl might mope otherwise, and there is no point in maintaining two homes when one will hold us all, is there?"

And smiling like a python that has swallowed a sheep, Mr Shugger led his son-in-law-to-be off the wharf; poor Martin stumbled along dazedly beside him, like the sheep that has been swallowed and still does not quite realize what has happened, while Jobbie went bounding along behind, taking a nip out of Martin's calf from time to time and chasing all the cats that came in sight. Wendy and her mother walked ahead, planning what they'd have for the wedding breakfast. Mrs Shugger was a terrible cook: even worse than Wendy; it was amazing that Minnie had been born into that family.

Well, late that evening, stuffed full of heavy soggy food which lay on his stomach like precast concrete, Martin went home to his own dear little cottage at number two, The Saltings — which he would have to himself for only two nights more. He lay on his bed, but he couldn't sleep; he was tossing and fuming, groaning and sighing, till daybreak. And what he mostly remembered were all the nights of his last voyage, after he'd posted off that fatal letter from Valparaiso, which had of course been intended for Minnie Shugger.

He remembered how, as he was taking night watch on the first night out from shore, he'd heard a voice from the shadowy water, which called out, "Martin? Is that you there, Martin?" and next minute, with a splash and a spring a smiling wet mermaid had bounced on board. Martin had never seen a mermaid before but anyway this one was quite different even from any that he might have imagined. For one thing, she was quite plump, and quite plain, too; she reminded him of somebody, but of whom he was not quite sure. She had light greenish-brown eyes, like the sea when sand is stirred up in it, straw-colored hair, and she was a bit freckled, but with nice white teeth, many of which showed when she gave him a big wide friendly grin and said, "How about a game of cat's cradle, Martin, to pass the night away?"

And she reached down behind her into the sea, pulled out a skein of silvery bubbling foam, and wove it into a loop, quick as I'm saying the words.

Down they sat, the mermaid comfortably propping her fat form against a pile of rope, and began to play. And before the night was out, Martin had learned two hundred and fifty new versions of cat's cradle, each different from the last.

"That's not all the ones I know, not by any means," said the mermaid. "I'll be seeing you again, Martin!" and with a swish of her plump tail, she dived overboard, just before Martin's relief came yawning on deck to take over the watch.

Each night, then, for ninety nights, the mermaid came on board to keep Martin company, and taught him new variations of cat's cradle as the old cargo ship wandered from port to port. But when the *Escallonia* came within sight of the Lizard Head, the mermaid said, "That'll be all for now, Martin; there's too much traffic in the Channel for my taste; I've no fancy to have half the scales scraped off my tail by the hull of an oil tanker; I'll be going back to open ocean again. See you next trip, Martin."

"How will you find me, though?" he asked.

"Never worry about that; I'll find you," the mermaid said. And before sinking out of sight, she tossed her skein of bubbles around Martin's neck, so that it lay light as a draft of cool air against his skin. Then she dropped under the surface of the waves. And what happened to Martin when he reached land, you have already heard.

Well, two mornings after Wendy's welcome, all dressed up in his black best and feeling just like a funeral, Martin was wed to Wendy Shugger, for he could see no way to escape from the business. There were dozens of Shugger relatives at the ceremony; aunts, uncles, and cousins; one uncle was a lawyer, another ran the bank, another was mayor of the town; Martin felt they were around his neck like a noose, and a very different one from his dear mermaid's noose of bubbles (which was the only thing that kept him even halfway cheerful as it lay cool as air under his shirt). All the Shuggers sat in the church, grinning their faces off, and followed the wedding procession home like a parcel of walking mushrooms.

And two days later — by which time, all Martin's hopes were pinned on getting back to sea at the very first opportunity — another blow fell, even worse.

Mr Shugger came in at noon — for Wendy's parents had lost no time in taking up residence at number two, The Saltings — clapped his son-in-law on the shoulder, and said, "well, no more dangerous ocean voyages for you, my boy! I've arranged you a job as spray-dryer superintendent at the soap factory; you can start tomorrow!"

"What?" cries Martin, his eyes almost falling out of his

head with horror. "But Cap'n Egg is expecting me in five days' time; he's given me the mate's berth."

"I've sent a message to Captain Egg telling him you won't be coming," said Mr Shugger. "So you don't need to worry about that. Now, what has Wendy got for our dinner? Ah, sausages — delicious!"

The sausages were like pale wet chopped-off sections of cable, and the mashed potato that went with them might easily have been mistaken for wallpaper paste; and after that came a dish of rhubarb so sour that Martin was amazed it had not eaten a hole clean through his gran's enamel pie dish.

That eaten, Mr Shugger led his dazed son-in-law through the door, along the street, and down a dreary back alley to the bit of waste land where his soap factory had been built.

"You can't learn the business too soon, my boy," he said. "*There's no time like the present, a stitch in time saves nine*, and *Satan finds some mischief still for idle hands to do*, so I'll just take you round and show you what's what. You climb up those steps and go along that catwalk; hold on tight, for it's narrow and the soap tends to make it slippery."

There was a terrible smell in the place, a mix of boiling fat, ashes, glue, seaweed, grease, and lime. Poor Martin nearly choked on it, and was so busy holding his breath that he hardly had time to attend to what his father-in-law was saying.

"Now, this is where we drop in the additives," said Mr Shugger, pointing downward. "And here, this is where we mix everything together, in this tank, which is called the batch crutcher, because it crutches the batches."

Martin gazed down into the horrible whitish-gray

swirling seething gooey porridge-like brew that was bubbling just down below the gantry they stood on, and his spir-
its fell so low that he'd half a mind to take a dive into the mix;
not quite, though; it did look so nasty.

"Now, from there," continued Mr Shugger, "it passes
through this affair, which is the cooling roll, and then it
moves along to the chip dryer, which makes rather a noise,
as you can hear, but you will easily be able to follow what I'm
saying if you can lip read.

"Now, here we come to the plodder, which is in three
stages. First there is the preplodder — this is it; then there is
the plodder proper — which is this; and lastly, there is the
final plodder. After that, we come to the amalgamator — here
it is, amalgamating everything that has gone before; then
there are the two mills — they do clank a bit, that is because
the soap gets into the joints, but they are highly necessary, I
assure you; and finally it all goes through the vacuum box, of
course. After that we come to the spray-drying tower, which
will be your province, Martin — that's it over there; and the
spray nozzler, you will have time to look after that too; this
here is the cyclone dust collector (soap dust is quite valuable,
we sell it all to Hottentots at two pounds a ton) and this is the
exhaust air fan. Those things over there are the fabric filter
socks — whatever you do, take care not to get your hand into
them.

"Now, are you quite clear about the whole process? Very
good, then you can start at nine o'clock tomorrow morning."

And he beamed at Martin before going off to inspect a
batch of soap which, for some reason, had not been properly
crutched in the batch crutcher.

Martin hurriedly escaped from the awful place before
somebody could ask him to darn the filter socks or shake out

the spray nozzler. He couldn't bear to go back home to his cottage, for Wendy was there with her mother and they had asked two aunts and six cousins to tea; he couldn't bear to go on to the dock, because there he would see his former ship, the Escallonia, being fitted out for sea; he couldn't bear to walk on the beach, because the mere sight of waves made him miserable; so he turned inland and walked up onto the moor behind the town.

Up and up he walked, and presently came to a little valley where a stream ran chuckling to itself between rocks. Martin sat down beside the stream; his heart was so heavy that if it had fallen into the stream it would have sunk like one of the rocks.

But his heart did not fall into the stream; what fell in was his skein of bubbles, which slipped from his neck and dropped into the water, leaving nothing but a faint momentary cool sensation that faded from his skin like a touch of breeze.

"Oh!" thought poor Martin sadly. "There goes my last link with my dear mermaid. Now I know that I shall never see her again." But in a way, he thought, sighing, it was just as well that he had lost his chain, for if Wendy laid eyes on it there would be the devil to pay — she would want to know where he got it, who gave it to him, and every last thing about it.

He stood up, stared gloomily down at the clear water, and then began walking slowly homeward, kicking at any stones that lay in his way. His hands were in his pockets, his head was bowed, and he did not once look behind him.

If he had, he would have seen that the stream had left its bed and was following at his heels like a faithful dog (or rather, like a faithful serpent).

When Martin reached the village, of course, people soon began to stare, for there was the stream just behind him, chuckling and bubbling to itself, following him closely along the street; arching up like a caterpillar, twining from side to side like a viper, wriggling like a centipede, tying itself in knots like a conger eel. Martin, so full of care that he neither saw nor heard it, came to the front door of his house at number two, The Saltings. There he had just lifted up his hand to turn the knob when the door flew open, to reveal his wife, Wendy, red with annoyance, her eyes darting sparks.

"I suppose you think it's clever to stay out half the day when I told you tea was at five and two of my aunts and six of my cousins here to meet you and I'd specially asked you to stop in at Blodgett's and bring half a pound of orange pekoe!" she snapped. Then she looked past him and gave a gasp; her face went white as cuttlefish bone. For the stream had arrived right behind Martin, and it reared up like a striking cobra; then it roared down on Wendy, wrapped itself three times around her neck, and carried her away, down the street, tossing Martin sideways onto his own doorstep as it did so. With its tail, it swept up the barking, snarling hysterical Jobbie and carried him along, too.

By the time Martin had picked himself up and given chase, the stream was out of sight with its captives, but Martin followed the sound of rushing water and its wet trail down the main street and along the dreary back alley as far as Shugger's soap factory. And there, what a sight met his eyes! The stream had gone raging through the factory, smashing the batch crutcher and turning it upside down on top of Mr Shugger, knocking all the dry soap into the amalgamator, bending the spray-drying tower into a hoop, blowing out the cyclone dust collector, buckling the exhaust air fan, tying the fabric filter socks into twenty knots, and finally dropping both Wendy and her dog into the middle plodder, where they were rapidly transformed into scouring powder.

Martin, seeing there was nothing to be done for them, walked straight to the wharf, where he found Captain Egg superintending the stowage of the last stores aboard the *Escallonia*.

"Is your mate's berth still vacant, Cap'n?" asked Martin.

"Certainly is, my boy, if you are free! I'd got in my nephew James, but he can serve as A.B. till next trip," said Captain Egg, beaming all over his face, for he was fond of Martin and had been sorry to lose him. "In fact, you may as well stay here now and help me check these stores."

Martin stayed with Captain Egg, and he slept on the ship and was so busy that he never went back to his house for three days. Then he found that Mrs Shugger had left and moved to a large mansion which she was buying with her husband's life insurance, not to mention the insurance from the wrecked factory. So, without speaking to her again (or any of the aunts and cousins), Martin collected his duffel bag and returned to the ship, which put to sea on that night's tide.

And the very first watch that Martin stood, there was the mermaid, fat and chuckling, with a new skein of silvery foam and a new variation of cat's cradle. "So my greedy sister tried to get you, did she, Martin?" says she. "I reckon you'll be more careful next time you address an envelope to a young lady when you are making her an offer of marriage!"

"I will that, Miss Wilhelmina," said Martin, and then they settled down to their crissc-ross game, while the waves pushed past underneath and the stars sailed by overhead.

Moonshine in the Mustard Pot

Deborah had been anxious about what she would find to do while staying with Granny. "Shall I take toys?" she asked, and her father said, "it's a very small house. Better not take much; there'd be nowhere to put them."

At home, in spite of having her own room crammed with toys, Deborah was bored as often as not, and would trail in search of her mother, yawning. "What shall I do, Mum?" And her mother, quick as lightning, always found her a job: tidy the spoon-and-fork drawer, polish the silver teapot, weed the moss out of the front steps. Not bad things in themselves, but jobs done to fill a gap are like going on your favorite walk with somebody who walks at the wrong pace; there's no satisfaction in them. Deborah never seemed to learn this, though; sooner or later she would be wandering back again, saying, "I'm bored; what shall I do?"

Granny's house, in a little street in York, certainly was tiny. The first thing Deborah noticed about it was that it sat flat on the ground: no front steps to climb (or weed). Somehow, inside, you could feel the earth, right there under the floor; it was a bit like going out in very thin-soled slippers. Her father said, "I hope I've brought enough warm clothes for her; I wasn't sure what to pack." Deborah's mother was sick; that was why she was here. "Well, if the weather gets cold, the child can wear my woollies," Granny said. "She's almost as big as I am."

It was true. Granny was small, suited to her house, thin and straight as a candle in her cotton print pinafore over two layers of jerseys. Her hair, fine and soft and white as smoke, she wore pinned back in a bun; and her face was white as well, so pale that Deborah feared at first she must be ill too, but no ill person could possibly be as energetic as Granny. "It's just old age," she explained about the paleness later. But the black eyes in this white face sparkled like two live coals; they were never still for a minute.

The minute Deborah's father had gone, Granny showed her over the house. There were four rooms and a pantry. The doors were so narrow that you could only just carry a chair through them. The stairs, equally narrow, led straight out of the kitchen through another tiny door. "Suppose you wanted to get a big piece of furniture up?" said Deborah. "Wouldn't have room to put it anywhere if I did," said Granny. "Besides, I don't like big furniture. I like things I can move myself. The biggest load isn't the best."

Indeed, all her things were small and light — stools, low narrow beds, tiny velvet nursing chairs. "Bought at auctions," said Granny with satisfaction. "Never paid more than a pound for anything yet. And I make sure I can lift it before I bid." She had painted and upholstered everything herself — clear soft blues, apple green, warm brick red, white, rose pink, purple, indigo, chocolate brown. The whole house sang and flashed with color.

"How did you paint the ceilings, Granny?"

"With a brush tied to a mop handle, of course. Never believe in getting in a man for jobs you can do yourself. Take days and make the fiend's own mess and charge double, the robbers. Now, I've just bought this little chest for the bathroom; I thought you might like to help me paint it."

"Oh, yes!" said Deborah. "What color?"

The bathroom was brand-new, Granny's pride: "Your Uncle Chris made it for me when he was home from India for a month. Didn't tell the Council. That the eye doesn't see, the heart doesn't grieve over. Oh, he's a clever one, that Chris." About the size of a kitchen table, the bathroom was tucked in a corner of Granny's bedroom. "Before, I had to go all the way to the washhouse." The washhouse was in the tiny garden, out at the back, across a brick-paved yard and also a narrow lane, which was a public right-of-way.

"Not very convenient when you want to brush your teeth," said Deborah.

"Oh, I did that in the kitchen sink."

"But what about in the winter, when it snows?"

"Well, you get used to anything."

But Deborah was glad Uncle Chris had made the bathroom. It was lined with dark blue tiles and had a white basin and toilet seat, so they decided to paint the chest scarlet, and it took them till lunchtime. "And after lunch, while it dries," said Granny, "I'll show you my allotment, where I grow my vegetables."

"Not your back garden?"

"No, that's for sitting in."

The back garden, past the washhouse and about the same size as the kitchen, had grass and four apple trees covered with young uncurling leaves and coral buds. "Apples off them lasted me all winter," said Granny. "Coxes, Laxtons, Bramleys, and Beauty of Bath." Deborah had never heard these names and now learned them in a jingle:

> *Cox and Laxton left of the path,*
> *on the right Bramley and Beauty of Bath.*

Granny fetched her bicycle out of the washhouse. It was painted apple green (the same paint as the kitchen dresser) and was so ancient that the back wheel was protected by a skirt guard of strings threaded from holes in the rear mudguard to the hub. A square hamper was strapped on the carrier. "For vegetables," explained Granny. She added a cushion on top of this and sat Deborah on top of the cushion; so they rode through the city of York to Granny's allotment, which lay out on the far side. Granny pedaled along at a spanking pace and the traffic kept respectfully out of her way.

"Granny," yelled Deborah through the mixed sun and wind and shadow of their headlong course, "can you explain something Dad said?"

"What was that, child?"

"He said, 'I hope Deb will be all right with her. Mother takes her life in her hands twenty times a day.'"

Granny swept the bike up to a hawthorn hedge covered with white blossom and a gate that led to the allotments.

"That's the way life ought to be taken," she said. "If you have your life in your hands, then you can steer it, can't you?

I wouldn't give a brass button for the sort of life that's just left lying around, like wet washing. Now, we'll do the hoeing and weeding first, then I'll introduce you to the bees." Hoeing and weeding was not at all dull, as Deborah had expected it would be, because in among her vegetables Granny had scarlet anemones and dark blue grape hyacinths and dark velvet brown wallflowers and clumps of primroses; there was always something beautiful to look at and smell. "I like them and the bees like them," said Granny. "Nothing but vegetables makes a dull garden."

Also, while they hoed, Granny taught Deborah some of what she called her gardenwork poems: "Bonnie Kilmeny gaed up the glen", "Where the pools are bright and deep", "Loveliest of trees the cherry now", "No man knows through what wild centuries roves back the rose".

"I have different ones for doing housework, of course, and different again for sewing and going to sleep. Everybody ought to have plenty of different sets of poems stowed away."

Deborah had never thought of poems as something you could have, like flowers or stamps or colored stones. "Of course you can," said Granny. "And the best of it is, that everybody can have them at the same time. And they cost no more than moonshine in the mustard pot."

"Moonshine in the mustard pot — what's that, Granny?"

"Why, nothing at all."

Granny was full of interesting proverbs. "If that was a bear, it would have bit you", she said when you were looking for something and it was right under your nose. "I'd rather have stags led by a lion than lions led by a stag." "He that would live forever must eat sage in May." "Ask a kite for a feather, she'll tell you she has only enough to fly with."

"Now you can come and meet the bees, but you must put on a hat first."

Secretly, Deborah was rather nervous of the bees, who lived in three square white hives by the hedge, but they seemed to be wholly busy helping themselves to nectar from the hawthorn blossoms. "This is their hard-work time," said Granny. "Well, all times are busy for bees, once the daffodils begin. — Of course they must get to know you. Don't you know that you have to tell bees everything?"

"What happens if you don't?"

"They pine and grieve and sing a sad song. And the honey tastes bitter. Or there is none. Besides," said Granny as they put on old panama hats draped with white veiling that made them look like Tibetan monks from Mount Everest, "your name — Deborah — means a bee, didn't you know? So that's a special reason for saying good afternoon to them."

She lifted off the tops of the hives like box lids, and Deborah, peering down through the drifts of her veil, saw the black-and-gold bees, more than any multiplication table could calculate, in their tireless to-and-fro. The combs, pale caskets of wax, were built between glass panels so that Granny could see how the honey was getting on. It glowed light and dark gold through the rind of wax, and the bees made a continuous murmur, a blend of all their different humming notes, with one steady note in the center.

"Perhaps that's the queen bee's note?" said Deborah.

On the bike ride home (they kept on their hats and veils for the ride and were the wonder of York) Granny taught Deborah a bees' poem:

Heavy with blozzomz be
The rozez that growzez
In the thickets of Zee.

After tea, Deborah helped Granny water and feed all her plants, of which she had about fifty, ten to each windowsill. She talked to them all the time she was attending to them, scolding and praising, telling them news of the plants in the other rooms and the garden. "They grow better if you do that," she explained. "Do you say poetry to them too?"

"You can do," said Granny, "but plants seem to like real news best. Sometimes I read the paper aloud to them. They do like music, it's true. And of course you have to listen to them as well."

"Listen?"

"In case they've got any grievances. Terrible ones for sulking, some plants can be."

When the plants were done, there was the starling to be given his lesson.

"When he first came to live here I could hardly abide him," said Granny. "Squawk, squawk. Not one decent sensible thing to say for himself. But Mr Jones (who's the music teacher at the Comprehensive and plays the piano in chapel on Sundays), he lent me a book of tunes you can teach birds. Hundred years ago, everybody was doing it. Now it's all television, nobody has time."

The starling, Jack, who had a lame leg, had been rescued by Granny from a cat and had decided to take up residence in her house. He came and went as he chose, through a hinged pane in the kitchen window, but spent most of his time sitting among the willow-pattern china on the green dresser. He was as glossy himself as a luster mug. "I will say for him, he's clean as a Quaker," said Granny. "I've never known him to clart the place but once, and then the curtains were drawn and he couldn't find his way out. Here's the book; do you want to teach him a tune?"

The book, which looked quite old, was called *100 Prettie Tunes to Teach Canarays or Other Cage Birdes*. But Deborah was obliged to confess that she could not read music.

"Can you not, child? Oh, well, I'll soon teach you that." And in half an hour she had. "See, it goes up and down along the stave — that one is "God Save the Queen" — Queen Anne it would have been, then, I daresay — so you can see how it works. And this note here, like a ball of wool on a knitting needle, that's *C*." She sang it in her thin, clear old voice. "But how do you know?" said Deborah. "Well, if you don't know, you can find out from the tuning fork," said Granny and took it out from a stone marmalade jar on the dresser, a thick *Y* of blue metal, "but you'll soon find you remember the note." Deborah found this was true. They began teaching Jack the first line of "Lillibullero," but quite soon he became tired and stuck his head under his wing. "You'd better go off to bed too, child," said Granny. "Oh, but I don't go to bed nearly as early as this at home," said Deborah. "No, but at home I daresay you don't get up so early," said Granny. "I'm always up at six and through the housework before breakfast, so as to have it out of the way for the day."

Deborah ate her supper in front of the kitchen fire: cup of cocoa, piece of dripping-toast, and the crusty end of the loaf spread thick with globby, homemade, yellow-plum jam.

"Now," said Granny, "you must choose your bedroom. The back one's bigger, and has the sun in the morning, and

looks over the garden, but then you have to come through
my room to get to the bathroom. Or, if you like, you can have
my room, and then you're right beside the bathroom — but
then I shall have to come past you — and I warn you, old
people are always getting up in the night. After seventy you
sleep with one eye open."

Deborah thought she would have the back room; she
didn't want to turn Granny out of her bed. Granny gave her
a small flashlight in case she needed to find her way to the
bathroom in the dark. Also an apple.

Eat an apple going to bed
Make the doctor beg his bread.

Perhaps because of the apple, or the cocoa, or the strange
bed, or because she had learned so many new things during
the previous day that her mind was buzzing with them like
all three beehives put together — Deborah woke after she
had been asleep about four hours, and sat straight up in bed.
Perhaps, after all, it was the moon that had woken her — a
bent square of light lay, half on the white wall, half on the
bluepainted floor. There seemed no need for her flashlight,
after all, but Deborah took it just in case Granny's room was
darker. She slipped out of bed onto the little braided rag rug
(made long ago by Granny, who had promised to show
Deborah how) and tiptoed across the shiny blue floor into
the other room. That was quite light too, with reflected
moonlight from the windows of the houses across the street.
There lay Granny, a small breathing shape, flat in her bed.
But the minute Deborah set foot in her room she sat bolt
upright, throwing off the covers. Her straight white hair, free

from its knot, hung around her face like a child's. Her eyes were fast shut.

"Who are you? And where are you from?" she said sharply. Her voice was different from her daytime voice — higher, and clearer too; a younger person's voice.

Deborah's heart battered against her ribs, like Jack the starling looking for his way out through the curtains.

"It's Deborah, G-Granny," she stammered. "I'm Deborah!"

Granny turned her impatient, sightless face toward the door, "No, who are you?" she snapped. "Who are you, I said — and where are you from?"

"But I'm Deb — your granddaughter Deborah. From — from home. From London."

"Who are you?" Granny repeated for the third time. "Where are you from?"

Deborah was so terribly daunted and abashed by this that she retreated on tiptoe from the doorway, back across her moonlit floor, and then jumped into bed and pulled the bedclothes tight around her chin. She was half afraid that Granny would come after her. Nothing of the kind had ever happened to her before. She felt terribly queer — as if she had found herself, by mistake, inside the egg of some strange bird who was shouting, "Trespassers will be prosecuted" in her ear. Or a mermaid's egg — do mermaids have eggs?

Luckily she had not wanted to go to the bathroom too desperately; before she knew it, she had slipped back into sleep.

In the morning, Granny was so exactly the way she had been yesterday, which seemed so just and precisely Granny-ish that Deborah could not imagine her ever having been different — she was so neat and active, so brisk and talkative, nipping about with a mop and duster while the kettle sang and the bacon frizzled — that Deborah plucked up courage and told what had happened in the night.

"You sat up in bed, Granny, as straight as a stick, and you said it in such a fierce tone that I was really frightened."

Granny couldn't help laughing at the story — in fact she laughed so much that she had to sit down on Deborah's blue bedroom chair — but when she had recovered she said, "That won't do, will it, now? We certainly can't have you frightened like that."

"Why do you suppose you didn't believe me when I said I was Deborah?"

"I daresay because it seemed too simple."

"How do you mean, Granny?"

"Well, when you're asleep you're much more than just plain Deborah, aren't you? You might be a princess or a fish or a tree or a horse or the moon or a whole lot of things one after the other — you're everything you ever dreamed you were, all baked together in a pie of sleep."

"But you were the one who was asleep, Granny — I was awake!"

"That's what I mean," said Granny. "If you're explaining to someone who's asleep, you've got to put it all in — not just the top layer. Do you see?"

"I'm not sure," said Deborah.

"Well, of course, the first thing is not to be scared if it should happen again. Just give me an answer. And if it isn't the right one first time, go on trying till it is. Or walk past. After all, I'm only your old Granny!"

"But suppose you're a fish or a tree or the moon?"

"Sit down and eat your breakfast, child — the bacon's getting cold. Cold bacon hot again, that love I never."

After breakfast they sides-to-middled some worn sheets — Granny let Deborah tear the old flimsy cotton, which gave with a scrumptious purring rip, like wood splitting but softer. Then the torn edges had to be hemmed and the outer sides joined together; Deborah turned the handle of the sewing machine while Granny guided the cotton under the bright, rapidly-thudding foot and the needle that flashed up and down. Then they changed over: Granny turned the wheel and Deborah learned to steer the material; it was more difficult than she had expected and she made some wild swerves before she mastered the knack, but, as Granny said, it all helped to strengthen the sheet and was good practice.

Then they added a bit more onto the patchwork quilt, which was, Granny said, the ninth she had made; it was already single-bed size but needed to be double, since it was intended for a wedding present. The pieces were six-sided, the colors mostly dark reds and pale green and cream color, but each corner contained a circle made up of all kinds of patterned bits and in these Deborah recognized pieces left over from several dresses that Granny had made and sent her in the past.

Then they whitewashed the inside of the washhouse using big brushes and buckets of distemper and getting so splashed that they had to have baths afterward. Then they bicycled down to the shops, singing "Pop Goes the Weasel," and bought half a pound of rice, which cost considerably more than twopence, and a jar of treacle, and Granny taught Deborah how to make a treacle tart. And then they ate it.

After lunch they went to the allotment and planted young leeks and sowed peas and two kinds of beans. "You'll have to come back to help me eat them," said Granny. "I don't want to go away from here, ever," said Deborah. On the ride back they went around by way of York Minster for Deborah to see it; the arched ceilings inside reminded her of Granny's patchwork quilt, except that they were creamy white, but they were covered with the same kind of patterns; and the windows were exactly like the inside of Granny's house; they gave just the same feeling — of somebody's having thought very hard, deciding which were her favorite colors, and then put every single one of them in.

That night, Deborah went to sleep almost before her head hit the pillow (Jack the starling had reamed another six notes of "Lillibullero," but it had been hard work); then the moonlight woke her, four or five hours later, shining like a T V screen on the wall opposite her face. She crept across her room and was halfway to the bathroom door when, as before, Granny woke and sat bolt upright in bed.

"Who's that? Who are you?"

"I'm a bicycle," Deborah said, guessing. Granny moved her head a little, frowning in her sleep, as if this might be the right answer but not all of it. "I'm the wind, I'm a street light, I'm a one-way street, I'm a zebra-crossing."

At each of these things, Granny nodded. "Where are you from?" she said.

"I'm — I'm from the other side of town," said Deborah, and made her escape into the bathroom. When she came out again, Granny was lying down fast asleep, and never stirred.

"There you are, you see!" she said triumphantly next morning. "I told you it was perfectly simple. All you have to do is say the right thing!"

That day they made new curtains for the kitchen (Granny had bought the material ten years before at a jumble sale and had been saving it for just this use; it was plain black-and-white stripes with, just here and there, a bunch of green grapes printed on the cotton); they sponged the shiny indoor plants, sowed some broccoli, and got ready a cold frame for pumpkins. They told each other stories. They bought a small, undressed doll at an auction (along with a stepladder, a jam caldron, and five large earthenware crocks) and began planning its wardrobe. Deborah learned how to make shepherd's pie. They picked big bunches of grape hyacinths and narcissi, which smelt sweet as honey all over the house.

And that night, when Granny said, "Who are you?" Deborah said, "I'm a needle, I'm a spoon. I'm a length of cotton. I'm a ladder, I'm a bird, I'm a window."

"Where are you from?"

"I'm from all around you, Granny."

Instantly Granny lay down, perfectly satisfied, it seemed, with these answers.

During the next month of nights they played this game many times in Granny's sleep. It was like fishing, Deborah thought — except that she was not quite sure who was the fish and who the fisher. Granny asked the question and Deborah threw out her answer like a line; sometimes it was right, sometimes wrong. If it was wrong, Granny would not have it. "I'm an apple, Granny." "No, you are not! Who are you, and where are you from?" Some nights, Deborah got it right at once, sometimes she had to feel her way slowly, guess by guess, cold, warm, warmer, until she hit the right answer. "I'm a line, a rope, a fish, a trout, an eel!" "And where are you from?" "From — from Newfoundland!" And where she got that answer from, goodness knows; but it seemed to satisfy Granny.

Of course, Deborah did not get up every night; sometimes, tired from all they had done and said and learned and thought, she slept clean through the silent hours of dark. But she often had a curious feeling on those nights, even more than after the ones when she had woken, that Granny had been asking questions and she had been answering them, without the need for words.

At last a letter came. Deborah's mother was better. And then her father came to take her home.

Deborah did not want to go. She wanted to stay so badly that it seemed probable no one but Granny could have persuaded her to get into the car with her father. "You'll be able to show your mother how well you can make a shepherd's pie and a treacle tart. And I'm going to give you these plants to look after for me, and you must write to me every single week and tell me how they are getting on."

Loaded with all the things she had made — the pair of slacks, the doll with two sets of clothes, the pot of lemon curd, the cake, the Japanese garden made from stones and moss in a foil piepan, the pincushion stuffed with dried coffee grounds, the clove orange — Deborah went home. "Why can't everybody be like Granny?" she wept, and her father, driving the car, said, "it's just as well everybody isn't, or there wouldn't be room to move in the world with all the things that got made and everybody bustling about," and he swerved his car to avoid an old lady who was bicycling along with a full basket.

In fact, Deborah settled down at home again not too badly. She had all her new skills to practice, and she kept up the habit of reading a new poem every day, and she wrote to Granny, with pictures, about the growth of the plants and about her new baby brother, and sent patchwork pieces, and sometimes a poem that she had written herself. Granny always answered right away, on a postcard. "Pieces v. useful. Glad to hear about the plants. Jack learned Danny Boy. Strawb. jam turned out well. Saving pot for you. Too busy to write more at present. *G.*"

The cards were always gorgeously colored. Granny got them from a bookshop near the minster; they were reproductions of pictures that had taken her fancy, and presently Deborah had half a wall full of them: battle scenes, flowers, landscapes, ships, angels, breakfast tables.

And then one day Deborah's father had a telegram:

YOUR MOTHER INJURED IN STREET
ACCIDENT. IN YORK HOSPITAL.
PLEASE COME.

"I always said she'd end up in trouble, riding that crazy old bicycle," he said, distractedly throwing socks and razor and pajamas into a bag.

Deborah got out her own bag and began packing it.

"No, no, dear, you can't go," said her mother. "It wouldn't be at all suitable. Children are only in the way when people are ill; it wouldn't do at all."

But Deborah was so absolutely ferociously determined — "Granny would want me. After all, I know how she does things; I'd know everything she wanted" — that in the end, somehow, without anyone actually having said *yes, you can go,* she was there in the car, driving to York with her father. "We'll go straight to the hospital," he said. "But you won't be allowed in to see her, I'm sure, so don't expect it."

"Why not?"

"Children never are allowed to visit sick people in hospitals."

"Why not?"

He didn't really know. "I suppose they'd bother the other patients."

"I wouldn't!"

"Well, anyway. . . . "

At the hospital they talked to a matron. It seemed the accident hadn't been Granny's fault: two cars had collided and one had bounced back onto Granny, who was coming up behind it on her bike. "I'm afraid she's very ill indeed," said the matron. "She may not know you." And there was absolutely no question of Deborah's being allowed in. She was told to wait in a dull empty room with nothing but a flat green bench and a smell of old flowers. Her father went with the matron, and Deborah sat wretchedly, kicking her heels against the legs of the bench and trying to say over one of the poems she had learned:

> *Where the bee sucks, there suck I*
> *In a cowslip's bell I lie . . .*

But this seemed no place for poems.

The worst of it was, she began to be certain that she could hear Granny's voice. So sure was she that she moved out of the waiting room and along a wide, huge, shiny corridor with doors all along each side. She listened, she walked a little farther, she listened again.

She came to a door that was not quite shut, and pushed it open a bit. And then she could definitely hear Granny's voice inside, with all its old impatience, saying, "No — who are you? Who are you?"

She heard her father's voice. "It's John, Mother. Don't you know me?" Granny's voice had been clear, but his sounded all choked up with worry and embarrassment.

Deborah put her head around the door. There were several people by a bed: doctors, she supposed, and nurses in white, and her father sitting on a chair. And Granny, trying to push herself up in the bed — at least it must be Granny because the white hair was certainly hers, but the face was mostly bandaged — and a nurse trying to persuade her to lie down again.

"No, but who are you?" cried out Granny, as if she could hardly bear all this stupidity, and Deborah, running to the bedside, said, quickly, before anybody could stop her, "Hullo, Granny! It's me — I'm a wing, I'm a flying leaf, no, I'm a bit of thistledown, I'm something high up and light, I'm a bird — no I'm a bee, Granny! I'm Deborah! I'm a bee!"

Granny turned her head toward Deborah's voice and listened keenly. Then she slowly settled herself back into a curled-up lying position, facing Deborah. A nurse tucked the clothes around, but she pushed them sharply off again, as if they bothered her.

"Deborah," she said. "That's it! You're Deborah. And do you know what you must do?"

"What, Granny?"

"You have to go and tell the bees, child . . . tell them. . . ."

"Yes, I'll tell them, Granny," said Deborah. Tears were running down her cheeks, which was silly, because of course the bees must be told; anybody knew that was the first thing that must be done after an accident or any important happening.

A nurse led her out of the room — there was a lot going on — and she was put in a different place to wait: someone's office. But Deborah was thinking about the bees. Really, they should be told at once; she slid down off her chair and walked to the end of the corridor, where she found a fire door and an outside flight of steps. She and Granny had passed the hospital once on one of their bicycle trips; she was pretty sure that she could find her way from there to the allotments.

The broad beans they had sown now dangled heavy pods, lumpy as Christmas stockings; some of the peas had pods, others were still in blossom. Marigolds and bachelors' buttons flashed among the rows of green. But the sun was gone by now; dew was falling. The sky was a pale oyster green. All but the most far-wandering bees had returned to their hives for the night.

Deborah knelt in the cold, dewy grass by the middle hive. She said, "It's about Granny. I think you ought to know. . . ."

Inside, the bees seemed to be listening. Their slumberous murmur had dwindled to a sigh that was hardly louder than her own breathing. And then she heard — or did she imagine it? — a tiny voice that might have been from the hives or from somewhere deep inside her own head, a voice imperiously demanding, "But who are you?"

"I'm Deborah," she whispered. And then she lay face down on the wet grass and cried her heart out. It was there that her father, scolding, anxious, harassed, and sad, finally found her.

"Did Granny die, then?" said Deborah.

She was quiet now, calmer than her father, who could only nod.

"Well, I expect it was best," Deborah said, after a minute.

"She would think it was better than not being able to ride her bike or dig in her garden or climb ladders, or any of the things she always did. Can you get someone to move her hives to Putney? Are there bee movers?"

"Move them to Putney? Are you crazy? People don't keep bees in Putney."

"Why not? Our garden's just as big as Granny's allotment. And there's all Putney Heath, too. We've got to look after Granny's bees; besides she left them to me; they're mine now. And you have to take care of bees; you can't just leave them to starve."

"I don't know what your mother will say. . . . "

But he knew she would get her way; as she had over the trip to York. On the way to London, while Deborah, curled in the back seat, taught lame Jack to whistle the first four bars of "Cherry Ripe," her father, driving the car, thought to himself, We've got another of them in the family now. She's going to be exactly the same.

The Wolves and the Mermaids

———◆———

There was once an old doctor, who lived alone with his cat, Jupiter, in the village of Ware-on-the-Cliff. There were only a few cottages, set in a gap overhanging the sea, and the doctor's house was on the very cliff edge. It was old and square, very large, and behind it lay a walled garden, protected from the furious sea winds. In the garden there were long walks and borders, yew hedges, a trellis covered with roses, and many fruit trees, but the curious thing was that all the trees were bare, the shrubs were leafless, and winter and summer alike not a plant or a flower grew out of the ground.

It had not always been so. When the doctor was younger, his son, Sam, had lived with him in the house. The son had learned to be a doctor too, but as there was no need for a pair of them in so wild a part, he earned his living by driving the bus which ran twice a day, morning and night, to the village of Ware-in-the-Woods. It was a long winding road between the two villages, more than a day's walk, and Sam was greatly blessed when he began driving his bus, for the way was very dangerous. Before the bus began to run, many a man had started out to walk it, and had never been seen or heard of again. This was on account of the wolves and the mermaids.

At first the road curved out along the coast, to avoid the great bare hill which rose behind Ware-on-the-Cliff, and all the way beside this coastal road were the waters where the mermaids sang and combed their hair and enticed travelers down into the sucking waves. Then the road turned inland and ran through a great forest which reached in all directions beyond anyone's knowledge. The forest was inhabited by myriads of wolves, so swift and fierce that if they scented a man he was doomed. But swift as they were, they could not overtake the bus, and loud though the mermaids sang, the roar of its engine was louder still, and so the people were able to travel from one village to the other in safety, and to go shopping and visit their relatives — a thing only the bravest had attempted before.

As for Sam, he was indifferent to both the wolves and the mermaids, for he carried a charm, a magic silver watch chain which would protect him from either beasts or men. Indeed, if the bus happened to be empty, he would often stop in the middle of the forest, and climb down from his cab, and go off hunting for rare plants and flowers among the trees. The wolves took no notice of him, and nobody minded if the bus was an hour late, for they knew that the plants he found were given to his father, who used them in the compounding of many healing ointments and drugs. Besides these, he brought home beautiful wild plants which he set in the garden, for he was a skilled gardener and when he was not driving he spent much time there, digging, raking, and pruning.

The flowers and fruits he grew were larger and more beautiful than any others in the two villages.

They were very happy living together, the father and son. They needed little, for the people whom the doctor cured mostly paid him in kind, a cake, a platterful of mackerel, or a dozen eggs, and this, with the vegetables that Sam grew in his garden, was enough for their wants. Old Jupiter would sometimes sit on the end of the pier which sheltered the fishermen's boats and scoop up a fine lobster or a crab, or bring them in a fat rabbit from the down.

In the mornings when the doctor was off on his rounds, Sam would come back from his first trip of the day and tidy up the house and make their midday meal. Then in the evenings, after the surgery which the doctor held in their kitchen, he went off for his evening trip, and his father would lean from the front door to shout: "Don't be late now. Sausages for supper!" and Sam, high in his cab, would wave and nod his head reassuringly.

But one evening, as the doctor looked out to wave goodby, he noticed that the end of Sam's chain was loose. He called out, "Mind your chain!" but his voice was drowned by the roar of the engine starting and Sam did not hear him. It was winter, and dusk was falling. The lights of the bus were on, but there were no passengers inside, and the doctor could see the rows of empty seats as the bus swung away up the cliff road. It was the last time he saw his son.

Whether the wolves caught him or the mermaids enticed him into the sea, nobody knew, for the bus did not come back.

And from that day the garden, which had been Sam's pride, began to wither and die away, the plants faded and then rotted into the earth, and the trees dropped their leaves and grew no more.

The people in the village were very kind to the doctor, bringing him gifts and trying to stop his grieving. He went on working even harder than before, and became more and more skillful at healing people's illnesses and wounds until he was spoken of with wonder in both villages.

A sum of money was collected, and a new bus was bought. The doctor drove it himself, for he felt so old and sad that he did not greatly care if the wolves or the mermaids caught him. If they ran or swam beside the bus he noticed them little more than flies.

But one evening when he was washing his hands after his surgery, before taking the bus out on the late journey, he felt a nudging and a pushing against his leg, and turning around was surprised to see a large gray wolf, who caught the doctor's sleeve in his teeth and began to drag him toward the door. The doctor was more puzzled than afraid, and he called to old Jupiter, the black cat. Since Sam's disappearance, the doctor and Jupiter had grown very close together and could understand each other very well.

He said now: "Ask him what he wants, Jupiter."

The wolf began to explain something in a pleading whine, scratching impatiently on the ground with his paw. At the end he again caught hold of the doctor's sleeve and tried to pull him out of the house.

"What does he mean?"

Jupiter explained to the doctor, by means of the sign language which they used, that the wolf wanted him to come to the aid of a friend who lay sick or wounded somewhere in the forest.

"Very well, tell him I'll come, but he must wait a moment while I get my bag."

When he was ready he went out and climbed into the cab of the bus, indicating to the wolf that he should travel inside. This the wolf was not very anxious to do, and only went in with many nervous starts. When the bus began to move he growled fiercely, but luckily there were no other passengers. The doctor took Jupiter with him as well, in case he needed an interpreter.

When they reached the middle of the forest the wolf tapped on the glass panel which separated him from the doctor, and made signs to him to stop. They got out, the doctor carrying Jupiter and his black bag, and the wolf plunged off the road and led them a long way until they reached a dense thicket of thorn and hazel. Here they found another wolf lying, desperately hurt, with more than a dozen wounds on his head, back and sides.

"You've been fighting," the doctor said severely, just as he did when Jupiter came in with a torn ear. The wolf, which was very weak, raised its bead a little and let it drop again; then the doctor quickly went to work, stitching some of the worst wounds, bandaging others, and applying his healing ointment.

"There," he said at length. "He'll be all right now. Make him understand that he's not to move for three days, and I'll come back then and have another look at him." Jupiter explained this with many lashings of his tail and whiskers. The guide wolf, which had meanwhile been sitting and watching attentively, now rose and licked the doctor's hand. Then he led them back to the bus, waited till it had started, and trotted back into the undergrowth again.

From this time on the doctor was quite often called in by the wolves. He learned that if two wolves fight, it is customary, if one becomes exhausted, for him to lie down on the ground and expose his defenseless throat to the conqueror. When he has thus acknowledged defeat he is spared by the winning wolf, and is allowed to get up and run away. It became usual in these cases, if the defeated wolf was badly wounded, for the victor to gallop off and fetch the doctor, who soon began to have a large practice among the wolves. As they had nothing to pay him with, he taught them to know the herbs and wild flowers he used, and then they found the places where these grew and took him there.

One moonlit night the doctor was driving slowly back through the forest from Ware-in-the-Woods, when there appeared on the road in front of the bus a wolf larger than any he had seen before. He pulled up, and as usual was led into the trees by the wolf, which every now and then glanced over its shoulder to make sure he was following. Each time this happened, he thought he saw a sort of gleam on its throat as if there were a white patch there, but he was not near enough to see it clearly, in that uncertain light. He found his patient, when they reached the hiding place, surrounded by a ring of wolves. They all stood up and bowed their heads when the doctor and his guide approached, making him realize that the large wolf must be the king of them all, who had nobly deigned to bring the doctor to a rival vanquished in combat.

The beaten wolf was very severely wounded, and it took the doctor a long time to make him comfortable. When he raised his head at last all the other wolves were gone; only the king remained to lead him back to the bus. The doctor was able to look at him closely for the first time, and then saw what he had mistaken for a gleam of white fur on the wolf's neck. It was Sam's silver chain.

For a moment he was struck dumb, and then pointing at it he stammered "where did you get that?"

The wolf did not understand, but Jupiter, who had accompanied the doctor, as he was now in the habit of doing, interpreted. The wolf made some explanation, which involved much waving of his tail and gesturing with his paw, and Jupiter explained that he had found it on the seashore, many months before, twined about a great shell.

"Since it is yours, you must have it back," the king wolf said, and lowered his stately head so that the doctor could remove the chain. He held it for a long time in his hands, looking at it as if he thought it could tell him where his son was. It seemed to him that this story must mean that Sam had been ensnared by the mermaids, and perhaps was not dead, but at this moment captive in some fastness under the sea.

From this time he began to feel a little spark of hope. He did not know how Sam might be saved, but he felt that somehow, perhaps it could yet be done. And the day after the king of the wolves had restored the chain, when he went into the garden, he found that on one rose tree a tiny bud had sprouted.

Some weeks later there had been fewer patients than usual at his evening surgery, and he had a little time before it was necessary to start the bus for the late trip. He went down and walked on the beach looking out to sea through the spring dusk.

Something moving on the breakwater caught his eyes as he strolled, and he turned and climbed the stone steps to see what it was. He found an albatross which had hurt its wing, and lay weak from lack of food, sheltered by the low wall. He took it back to his house to set the broken bones, and fed it some of the fish which Jupiter had caught for his supper. Then, locking it in his bedroom for fear of the cat, he set out on his evening journey.

The albatross stayed with him for several days, until he judged that the wing was fully recovered. On the fifth day it was as strong as ever, and he took it to the end of the pier and let it loose. It circled around him once and then flew straight out to sea.

That night, as he sat at his lonely supper, he heard a tap at the window. It was a gentle tap, but it turned him cold with fear, though he had thought he was no longer afraid of anything. He slowly crossed the room, raised the casement, and looked out, into the greenest and clearest eyes he had ever seen. They were set slanting in a white face, which rested on two long-fingered white hands.

His heart beat quickly and softly. "What do you want?" he said.

"You must help me." Her voice was like the soft, mournful whisper of the tide when the sea is far out, almost out of sight across the sand.

"If I can."

"You healed my albatross," she said, "so perhaps you can heal me."

He turned automatically across the dark room to find his black bag, and saw Jupiter in a corner, stiff with fear, every hair on end. Picking up the bag, he came back to face her again.

"What is your trouble?" he asked.

"A broken heart."

"Ah," said the doctor sadly, "if I could mend that, I should have mended my own. Nothing can cure a broken heart, my friend, except the person who broke it."

"But he never will," she answered, "for he hates me. Day after day I sing to him, I bring him the rarest treasures of the sea, but he sits grieving for his father and his lost garden, and never listens to me or looks at me."

The doctor's heart gave a great throb at this, but he only answered gently, "there is no cure for you, my friend. I cannot help you."

She sighed — a long sigh like the breaking of a wave on a windless day.

"Yet you healed my albatross," she said presently, "and I must repay you for that. What reward do you ask?"

"May I ask for anything?"

She bent her head in reply.

"Then give me back my son."

For the last time her sad green eyes looked into his, and then she turned and beckoned him to follow her. They went down the winding cliff steps to the shore, and there the doctor untied and dragged down his little boat, beached for so many months. She waited for him by the water's edge, and then turned and swam straight out to sea, while he rowed slowly after her into the dark.

It seemed to him that they went on for hours, until his arms and back were so tired that he could no longer feel them. But presently as he glanced from time to time over his shoulder, he thought that he could see a shadowy light glimmering through the water, and this became brighter and closer, until at length he could look down and see the whole ocean floor illuminated below him. There, fathoms down, was the bus, encrusted now with pearl, covered with waving plants and coralline growths of every color. And in the cab, imprisoned, tied with a rope of seaweed — was it?

"Sam!" he called, and the sound of his voice set off the ripples, shimmering away from the boat in every direction. His guide had dived down, and now with a stroke of her shell knife set Sam free from his bonds. The doctor leaned over the side of the boat and stretched down his hand to take his son's.

"Sam!"

"Father!"

The doctor turned the boat toward the shore.

"Let me row," said Sam, "you're tired." They moved slowly away into the darkness again, heading for the coast. All the way they were accompanied by the sweetest, most sorrowful singing that the doctor had ever heard, until it gradually died away out to sea, and the lights of the village began to show on the cliff.

"Nearly home, my son," said the doctor. "And it's sausages for supper."

John Sculpin and the Witches

One day John Sculpin's mother said to him: "I must wash my hair. Run down to the wishing well and fetch me a bucket of water."

"All right, Ma," said John, and he put on his beautiful cap, because it was raining and pouring torrents.

"And whatever you do," she said, "don't let a witch get that new cap of yours, because it's just the thing one of the old scarecrows would like, and I can't afford another one, let me tell you."

"How am I to stop her taking it, Ma?" asked John.

"If I've told you once how to get rid of a witch I've told you twenty times," said his mother. "Don't let me hear another word from you. Off with you."

So John went off, but whether it was from stupidity, or whether he just hadn't been listening, he couldn't for the life of him remember anything his mother had ever said to him about dealing with witches. And that was a pity, because, as it happened, the country around about there was infested with them.

John went along the road, thinking and thinking, and after a while he met an old woman.

"Afternoon, John," she said. "You look fretted about something."

"So would you be," said John. "My ma's told me the way to get rid of a witch, and I've clean forgotten it."

"If I tell you, will you give me that fine new cap you're wearing?" she said. John didn't like parting with his fine new cap, but the information seemed worth it, so he handed it over.

"Well," said the old woman, "all you have to do is give her a nice bunch of parsley."

"Of course, that was it!" said John. "I'll forget my own name next."

He thanked the old woman and went on down the road. The next house he came to was his uncle Sam's, so he went into the garden and picked a nice bunch of parsley. Then he walked down to the wishing well.

When he came up to the well, there was an old woman sitting beside it in the rain and muttering to herself. John went straight up to her and handed her the parsley, and she took it with a bit of a grunt and vanished; she'd gone to hang it up in her scullery.

John filled his bucket and went home. He put it down with a clank inside the back door, and his mother called out to him from the kitchen: "Did you see a witch?"

"Yes," said John, "there was one sitting beside the well, but I gave her a bunch of parsley and she took herself off."

"That's a good boy," said his mother. 'There's nothing like that wishing-well water for washing your hair in, I do say. Bring it in here, will you, with the big kettle."

When John went in, the first thing she said to him was: "Where's your cap?"

"Oh, I gave it to an old woman," said John. "She told me the right way to get rid of a witch."

"You little misery!" screamed his mother. "What's the use of telling you anything? You've given your cap to a witch, and not another one do you get till Christmas."

About a week later John's mother said to him: "We've finished all the potatoes. You'll have to go over to Malden's Farm and get a sackful. And this time, if you meet a witch, maybe you'll have the sense to give her a bunch of parsley right away."

So John fetched out his bicycle and pumped up the tires and found an old potato sack. And before he started he picked nearly a whole sackful of parsley and took it with him over his shoulder. It was about five miles to Malden's Farm, and the whole way, whenever John saw an old woman on the road, he got off and gave her one of his bunches of parsley. He wasn't taking any chances. Plenty of them looked a bit surprised at being given some parsley in the middle of the road, but that made no difference to John. By the time he had reached Malden's he had been so generous with his parsley that he had none left, and when he got to the farm gate and saw another old woman sitting outside he didn't quite know what to do.

"Haven't you anything for me, dearie?" the old woman asked.

John was a bit embarrassed, so finally he gave her the bicycle pump, as that seemed to be the smallest thing he could part with. Then he got his potatoes and went home.

When he came up the garden path his mother called from her bedroom window: "Got the potatoes, John?"

"Yes, Ma," John shouted back, "a whole sackful."

"But are they good ones?" she said, and came down to see. The first thing she said, when she came into the shed where John had put them was: "Where's the bicycle pump?"

"Well you see, Ma," John explained, "I'd finished all the parsley, giving it away to old women, by the time I got to Malden's. So I had to give the pump to the last one. Very pleased with it, she was. You should have seen her."

"You little good-for-nothing," screamed his mother. "What do you think we're going to do without the bicycle pump? Not another penny do you get to buy sweets till you've paid for a new one."

After that, all the witches in the neighborhood got to know about John, and they plagued him so much that he never dared stir out of doors without about half a cartload of parsley. So one day his mother said to him: "I've thought of a plan to get rid of the witches, and for goodness' sake, listen to what I'm saying, instead of mooning out of the window."

Next day she went all around the village saying: "My John's going to town. Have you any messages you want done?"

By the time she got home she had a list of messages as long as her arm, and all the witches knew that John was catching the nine-eighteen train into Tabchester the next day.

The porter always used to say that he'd never seen such a sight as there was that day. The station wasn't very big, and it was crowded from one end to the other with witches, all waiting for the nine-eighteen to come in. Some of them bought tickets and some didn't. John came a little late with his shopping basket and list. He went and had a private talk with the porter, who was also the stationmaster, and the guard, and the engine driver. Presently the porter (whose name was Mr Sims) went off and brought along the train. It wasn't a very big one, for it only went as far as Tabchester. There was no one else in it but John and the witches.

When the train began to move John got up and made a little speech. "Ladies," he said, "I didn't think I could bring enough parsley for all of you, so I've arranged a little treat for you, and you'll find it in the dining car at the end of the train."

So he went along the corridor to show them the way, and all the witches came pushing along behind him, rubbing their hands.

At the end of the train the corridor bent around, and there was a door to join on to another coach, if one should ever be needed. So John stood at the corner, and as each witch came around, he pushed her through the door and off the end of the train, and that was the end of her. All except the last. For the last but one, when he pushed her through the door, gave a kind of squeak, and that warned the one after her. So, quick as a wink, she changed herself into a bluebottle, and when John looked around, he thought he must have finished them all.

He went into the town and did all his errands, and when he got home he and his mother had a good laugh, thinking about all the witches.

But the last witch went home in a frightful temper, thinking how she could be revenged on John.

One day she put on a tweed cap and a false moustache and got on her bicycle and went off with a box on her back. And when she came to John's mother's cottage, she knocked at the front door and asked if they wanted to buy any toothbrushes. John's mother didn't recognize her, and she bought a new toothbrush for John. But the witch had poisoned this toothbrush, so that when John brushed his teeth with it, he would drop down dead on the spot.

But you know what boys are, even if the witch didn't. John never brushed his teeth in a month of Sundays. The first night he gave the brush a bit of a rub along the scullery draining board, to make it look used, and then he stuck it up on the shelf, and that was that.

Next morning his mother called: "John! Whatever have you been doing on the draining board? It's all black."

John came and looked, and sure enough, the board looked as if something like a black stain had been rubbed along it.

"I'm sure I don't know," he said, "unless it was my new toothbrush?"

He took it down and looked at it. Just then a fly came and settled on it, and the next minute it fell off onto the floor, as dead as a doornail. John and his mother looked at each other.

"A witch did that," said his mother. "You must have left one of them out, and she's got a spite against you. I'll be on the lookout for her the next time she comes selling things to me, the artful old besom."

A few days later the witch saw John coming down the road as well as ever. So she ground her teeth and began to think out a new way of getting rid of him.

Next morning she came riding up to the cottage in the uniform of a district nurse. "Morning, Nurse," said John's mother. "There's no one ill here, I'm thankful to say."

"Oh, I heard your little boy was ill," said the witch.

"It's more than I heard," said his mother. "But you can see for yourself."

For John came around the corner with a bundle of fagots.

"Oh dear yes, he's terribly ill," said the witch. "I can see it by the way he walks. You must put him to bed at once. I'll give you some medicine for him."

John's mother was a bit worried at that, and she hustled him into bed. That afternoon the witch came back with a little red bottle of medicine.

"You give him that," she said, "and we'll have no more trouble with him."

John's mother poured it into a glass, but you know what boys are. The minute her back was turned he poured the whole glassful into a jam jar full of honeysuckle on the washstand.

Ten minutes later she came back.

"Good gracious, John!" she said. "Whatever's happened to that honeysuckle? It's all black and shriveled."

"It must have been the medicine," said John. "I poured it into the jar."

"That's that witch again," cried his mother. "I'll lay for her the next time she comes pretending to be the district nurse. But the next time I catch you pouring your medicine down the sink or anywhere else, there'll be trouble."

A week later the witch saw John cycling through the village, and she nearly burst with rage. She thought and thought, but she simply could not think of anything nasty enough to do to him. While she was thinking, however, she nearly plagued the lives out of John and his mother in small ways. For they'd wake up in the morning to find nothing but giant vegetable marrows growing in the garden, or the tap would start running in the middle of the night and they would come down to find the kitchen flooded.

"It is so distressing," said John's mother to a friend of hers. "You never know whether you are on your head or your heels."

"There's only one thing to do when a witch starts plaguing you like that," said her friend. "You ought to pour a bucket of water over her, that's been taken from a running stream less than seven minutes before. Then she turns into a black cat."

Well, in the next three days John was fairly exhausted. He spent the whole of his time running backward and forward to the stream with buckets. And, of course, the witch never turned up.

But on the fourth day a smart young man came up the garden path, selling fine new dish mops. He had a whole bunch of them in one hand.

"Aha," said John to himself, "I've got you now." He stood behind the door with his bucket and waited for the young fellow to knock.

But as a matter of fact, the young man was a real salesman, and if John had looked out again he would have seen the witch herself, sneaking up behind him with a carrier bag full of scorpions, which she meant to put in the copper to surprise them. John never looked, though, and when a knock came at the door he popped out and flung the whole of the bucket over the young man, and then ran for his life. It was lucky he did, too, for the man was in a terrible temper when he picked himself up.

The first person he saw was the witch, who was laughing enough to split her sides. Of course, he thought she had thrown the bucket, and he gave her such a clout with his dish mops that he knocked her spinning into a clump of nettles. Then he took himself off, muttering such things under his breath that John's mother's black spaniel turned quite white to hear them.

But John and his mother were looking out of the side window to see what happened, and when they saw the man go off, and that he hadn't turned into a black cat, they thought that something must have gone wrong and the spell hadn't worked. So without waiting to see more they packed up all their belongings in the tablecloth and cleared out as fast as they could go.

The witch went home, grumbling and cursing, and after that, she wasn't nearly so lively about making herself a nuisance to people.

John and his mother settled down in a different part of the country where there weren't so many witches; which they might as well have done at first.

The Night the Stars Were Gone

There was once a boy called Tony whose father had a tree farm. Young trees of every sort in the world grew on his farm: oaks, palms, banyans, gum trees, coal trees, and Christmas trees. When the trees had reached a certain size, they were sold and taken away to be planted in parks or in gardens, or to make avenues or plantations.

Tony worked with his father and helped him feed and water the trees, and clip and trim and prune them so that they grew straight and sturdy. When people bought trees, it was often Tony who carefully dug them up and wrapped them in wet cloth and loaded them into a pony cart and drove them to wherever they were to be planted. Very often, it was he who planted the trees in their new places, so as to be sure they had a proper start.

One day, Tony had to take five young handkerchief trees to be planted in the garden of Lord Stone, a very wealthy man who lived in the nearby town.

As it happened, Tony had never been in Lord Stone's

garden before. When he arrived there, he thought that it was a very strange place. A huge iron gate was opened for him so that he could drive through. The garden was hidden inside a wall as high as a house. And it was all paved with stone; there were no lawns or flowers, not a single blade of grass. Trees grew here and there, in small square spaces, with ivy covering the soil around their roots. But the trees were not beautiful; they seemed like sad, stooped people, all twisted and knotted and gnarled; they looked as if they were not comfortable in Lord Stone's garden.

Tony felt unhappy for his five little handkerchief trees, with their big white leaves that looked as if they were meant for blowing noses or for fluttering in the breeze. He did not think they would like it in this silent, windless spot. But Lord Stone had bought the trees and paid for them, so Tony planted them as carefully as possible, spreading out the roots and giving them plenty of tree food, in the five new square spaces that had been made ready among the stone paving slabs.

While he was working, Tony noticed that a swing hanging from one of the twisted trees, was all studded with real pearls. And he could see a gold-paved swimming pool, and a silver climbing frame, and a seesaw with ruby seats. But in spite of these treasures, Tony thought that the garden was an ugly and gloomy place.

Then a girl came out of the house and watched him plant the last tree. She was younger than Tony, but very fat. She carried an emerald-studded hoop and a pair of roller skates with diamond buckles, but she did not roll the hoop or skate on the skates. She sat down on the iron chair and scowled at Tony, who thought she looked very bad-tempered.

"My father is much richer than your father," she said. "He is the richest man in the town."

"I know," said Tony.

"He is probably the richest man in the world."

"Fancy that," said Tony.

"He bought those trees to remind him of my mother, who is dead," said the girl.

"I'm sorry about that," said Tony, but the girl took no notice of his words.

"This whole garden is in memory of my mother," she said.

Tony did not know what to say to that. He loaded his tools into the cart.

"My name is Ann," said the girl.

"Oh," said Tony. She did not seem to want to know *his* name, so he did not tell it.

"Well? Do you like our garden?" said Ann.

"No, not very much," said Tony.

"Then, I think you are very rude," said Ann, frowning till her eyebrows nearly touched her fat cheeks.

A tall thin man came out of the house to inspect the trees. His face reminded Tony of the stone pavement, it was so set and flat and gray; his eyes seemed to look through holes like the holes in a mask.

"Don't talk to the garden boy, Ann," he said.

Ann put out her tongue at Tony and walked slowly toward the house. As she passed the cart, she gave the pony a thump with her hoop. Tony thought she was the fattest and most disagreeable girl he had ever seen. He was glad to leave the garden and go home to his father's farm.

But, after that, whenever his errands took him through the town, he tried to drive past Lord Stone's gates so as to look through the bars and see how his little handkerchief trees were getting on. They grew, but very slowly, and their white leaves hung down sadly. The wall around the garden was so high that the trees growing there were nearly always in shadow; the sun shone down on them only for an hour at noon.

As time passed, Tony noticed that many new treasures were brought into the garden: a rainbow in a glass box, a fountain of red wine; a rocking horse carved from white marble, with a gold saddle; a table carved from mother-of-pearl; an ivory summerhouse with beautiful pictures painted on its walls; and a garden parasol made from green jade and peacocks' feathers; but still Tony thought that the garden was a strange, sad place.

Sometimes, when he drove slowly past on his cart, fat Ann would come and put her tongue out at him through the bars of the gate. But she never said anything to him. Once or twice, Tony saw Lord Stone wandering slowly about the garden or going into the house. Often, Tony wondered what the inside of the house could be like; if there were such precious and costly things in the garden, what kind of furniture could they have indoors?

One evening, Tony was driving home just at sunset, down the long gentle hill that led through the town to the valley where his father's farm lay.

Tony loved this road at this time, for usually the sunset sky would be all pink and red and scarlet, with clouds like rose-colored or golden feathers. But on this evening the sky was strangely gray and empty, and the sun dropped out of sight with none of the usual sunset colors.

Tony might not have thought more about this if he had

not happened to notice, when he passed Lord Stone's gate
and looked through, that the windows of the big house, generally so dark and blank, were today all filled with pink light,
as if they reflected the sunset sky. And yet there were no sunset colors in the sky.

"That's queer," Tony thought.

But he drove home and did not think about the matter
again until the next evening, when he stepped out of doors
just after dark to take the pony her night feed.

There was the moon, shining white up above, but there
were no stars in the dark blue; not a single star to be seen
anywhere in the sky.

"Father!" called Tony in a fright. "Come and see! Someone's taken the stars!"

"Nonsense," said his father, looking for a moment and
then going back indoors; "it's cloudy, that's all. Come and
get your supper."

Tony went in, but he was sure that something was wrong.

The next night, the stars were still missing, and the night
after.

Tony asked several people in the town if they had noticed
that there were no stars.

"Oh," said one, "we've been having a lot of mist lately,
that's all it is."

"It's the time of the month," said another.

"It's the time of year," said a third.

"It's heat haze," said a fourth.

"Don't be silly," said a fifth. "You can't have looked properly. The stars are always there."

But the stars were not there in the sky, and Tony thought
he could guess where they might be.

So on the following night he climbed quietly out of bed

at midnight, when everybody was fast asleep, and he put on his clothes and walked across the town to Lord Stone's iron gates and looked through.

What a sight he saw!

The garden was full of stars: they hung in the boughs of the trees, quite weighing them down. They lay sparkling in the little square plots of ivy around the trunks of the trees. They were floating in the gold swimming pool, thick as breadcrumbs; and hundreds of them had collected, like midges, on the peacock-feather parasol.

By the flickering, twinkling light they gave, Tony could see that fat Ann was sitting on her iron chair among all those stars, and she saw Tony.

She walked to the gate and opened it and let him in.

"Well?" she said proudly. "Do you like our garden now?"

Tony saw that the windows of the house were all pink, still, with reflected sunset, although it was the middle of the night. Up above, the white moon hung in the empty sky.

"How did you get all the stars down out of the sky?" Tony asked.

"A traveling man sold my father a pair of long black gloves. If you put them on, you can reach anything that you want, anything in the world. So my father put them on, and reached up, and scraped all the stars down out of the sky."

"He shouldn't have done that," said Tony.

"What business is it of yours?" Ann said angrily. "The stars don't belong to you."

Then she started. "Oh!" she whispered. "Here's Father coming. He'll be angry that I let you in. Go away, quick!"

But Tony did not want to go. He waited till Lord Stone came up to them.

"Sir," he said. "You should not have taken the stars."

Lord Stone looked gray and tired in the flickering star-light. "Be quiet, boy," he said. "I am not interested in what you think."

He did not seem surprised or angry at finding Tony in the garden so late at night He kept rubbing and twisting his hands, pulling at the fingers of the long black gloves he wore, which went right up to his elbows.

"These gloves are too tight," he said. "As you are here, boy, you can help me pull them off."

Tony pulled at the gloves. But they were so tight that they seemed almost like skin. They would not come off. Lord Stone cried out with pain.

"Stops My hands feel as if they were burning!!"

"If you put your hands in the pool and wetted the gloves, that might stretch them," suggested Tony.

"I wish I had never bought the gloves," Lord Stone muttered. He dipped his hands in the pool, among all the floating stars. "What good does it do, anyway, to have all these stars in the garden? They don't bring my wife back. What is the use of them?"

Tony pulled again at the wet black gloves. But still they clung as tight as skin and would not come off.

"Now I remember," Lord Stone said. "The man from whom I bought the gloves said that if I wanted to get rid of them, I must sell them again, at the same price I gave for them. Boy, will you buy them?"

Tony did not want the gloves at all, but still, he felt sorry for Lord Stone. Very slowly, he said, "What price did you give for the gloves, sir?"

"All the money I had in the world," said Lord Stone.

"All I have in the world is a shilling," said Tony, "as I

help my father for nothing. But you can have that if you like." He took the shilling out of his pocket and handed it to Lord Stone.

Then they were able to pull the gloves off.

But Lord Stone's hands were still very painful; they burned and stung as if he had laid them on hot iron.

"Oh, if only there were some snow here," he cried. "If I could dip them in snow, I believe they might get better. Boy, you could reach out in the gloves and get me a bit of snow."

"No, sir," said Tony. "I bought the gloves from you, but I am not going to put them on. You must find your own snow."

"I'll go to the mountains," said Lord Stone. "I'll get out my car and drive there. Ann," he said to the girl, "will you come with me?"

"No," she said sulkily. "I don't want to go."

Lord Stone rolled up an ebony door in the wall and got out his enormous car and drove away in it without looking back.

The two long black gloves lay on the pavement like lizards between Tony and Ann.

"Why don't you put them on?" said Ann. "You could have anything in the world that you want to reach for."

"I don't want anything," said Tony.

He tied the gloves around a dead branch that had dropped from one of the trees, and carried them back through the moonlit streets to the edge of the town, to the corner of the valley where he and his father burned all their dead leaves and pruning and weeds and garden rubbish. A great fire was always slowly smoldering there, with a red-hot heart and a plume of blue smoke drifting away from it into the air.

Tony poked the dead branch, with the gloves wound

around it, right into the middle of the bonfire and covered
them with dry leaves and grass. They caught light at once
and burned fiercely, with a green flame and a black smoke.
They went on burning for a long, long time. As the green
flame slowly died down, Tony noticed something out of the
corner of his eye. He looked up and was just in time to see a
single star spring into the sky. Then three more suddenly
sparked out as if they had been switched on. Then thirty.
Then three hundred. Then three hundred thousand.

Next week, a neighbor said to Tony's father, "Have you
heard? No one has seen Lord Stone for a week. He went off
in his car and hasn't come back."

Tony began to wonder if Ann was all right. "Perhaps I
should go and see," he thought. He had to take two tree
lupines to a house on the far side of the town that afternoon,
so he came back by way of Lord Stone's gates and looked
through.

He noticed that grass had broken through the stone pavement. The slabs were cracked, as if they were hundreds of
years old. Spring bulbs, snowdrops and daffodils, were pok-
ing through. Some of the trees were in blossom.

The gate stood open, so he went in.

All the garden's treasures were gone: the pearl swing and
the marble rocking horse, the summerhouse and the rainbow
in a glass box. The pool water was rusty and full of dead
leaves. But the five little handkerchief trees looked sturdy
and well; they were covered with new buds.

Tony walked up to the windows of the house, which were
no longer full of pink light but were just plain glass, some of
them cracked. He looked through and saw that the rooms
inside were bare: no tables, no chairs, no rugs, no pictures,
nothing. Ann sat inside on the floor.

When she saw him she came out of the house. "What did you do with the gloves?" she asked.

"I burned them," he said. "In our bonfire."

"What is a bonfire?" she asked.

"Haven't you ever seen one?"

"No, never," she said. "Can I come and see it?"

"Of course," Tony said. "You can ride in the cart."

So he drove her back to the farm, and Ann looked at the bonfire, and the sheds full of tools, and the plow, and all the little growing trees.

Tony said, "Would you like to stay with us? Until your father comes back?"

"Could I?" said Ann. "Wouldn't your father mind?"

"No, of course not!" said Tony. "Come along in to supper."

He stabled the pony and took Ann up to the farmhouse. As he opened the back door, Ann said, "What is your name?"

The Boy with a Wolf's Foot

———•———

Once when I was traveling on a train from Waterloo to Guildford I looked out of the window and saw a boy and a great Alsatian dog running through the fields. Just for a few moments they seemed to be able to run faster than the train.

This is that boy's story.

The night of Will Wilder's birth was one of rain and gale; the wind went hunting along the railway embankment between Worplesdon and Woking like something that has been shut in a cave for twenty years.

Have you ever noticed what a lot of place names begin with a *W* in that part of the world? There's Wandsworth and Wimbledon, Walton and Weybridge and Worcester Park; there's Witley and Wanborough and West Byfleet; then, farther east, Waddon and Wallington, Woodmansterne, Woodside, Westerham, Warlingham, and Woldingham; it's as if ancient Surrey and Kent had been full of the wailing of wild things in the woods.

Maybe it was the wind that caused the train derailment;

anyway, whatever the cause, young Doctor Talisman, who, tired out, had fallen asleep in his non-smoking carriage after coming off duty at the Waterloo Hospital, was woken by a violent grinding jerk and at the same moment found himself flung clean through the train window to land, unhurt but somewhat dazed, in a clump of brambles that luckily broke his fall.

He scrambled through the prickles, trying to rub rain and darkness from his eyes, and discovered that he was standing, as it were, in a loop of train. The middle section had been derailed and sagged down the embankment, almost upside down; the two ends were still on the track. People were running and shouting; lights flared; the rain splashed and hissed on hot metal; the wind howled over all.

Pulling himself together the doctor made his way to the nearest group.

"I'm a medical man," he said. "Is anybody in need of help?"

People were glad to turn to him; there were plenty of cuts and bruises and he was kept busy till the ambulances managed to make their way to the spot — which took time, for the crash had happened quite a long way from the nearest road, and past stacks of timber and bricks, through a bit of dark countryside that was half heath, half waste land, with the River Wey running through it.

"Any seriously hurt?" an ambulance attendant asked, finding the young doctor working among the injured.

"One broken leg; several concussions; and there's one man killed outright," said the doctor sadly. "What makes it worse is that he had a young baby with him — born today I'd guess. The child's all right — was thrown clear in his carry-cot. Hasn't even woken."

At that moment the baby did wake and begin to cry — a faint thread of sound in the roaring of the wind.

"He'd best come along with us," said the ambulance man, "till we find someone to claim him. Hear the wind — hark to it blow! You'd think there was a pack of wolves chasing along the embankment."

Police and firemen arrived on the scene; the doctor was given a lift back to his home in Worplesdon. Next day he went along to the hospital where the injured people had been taken, and inquired after the baby.

"It's a sad thing," the matron said, "We've found out his father had just fetched him from the London hospital where he was born; his mother died there yesterday. Now the father's dead too the child has no relations at all; seems to be alone in the world. They'd just come from Canada, but had no family there. So the baby will have to go to the orphanage. And there's another queer thing: one of his feet is an odd shape, and had fur growing on it; as if the poor child hadn't enough bad luck already."

Young Doctor Talisman sighed, looking at the dark-haired baby sleeping so peacefully in his hospital cot, still unaware of the troubles he had inherited.

"I'll call in at the orphanage from time to time and see how he goes on," he promised. "What's his name?"

"Wilder. Will Wilder. Luckily we found his birth certificate in the father's suitcase. What are you looking for, doctor?"

"I was just wondering what I had done with my watch," Dr. Talisman said. "But I remember now: I took it off when I was helping to pull people out of the wreckage last night and buckled it to the branch of a tree growing on the embankment; I'll go back and find it sometime."

True to his word, the doctor called at Worplesdon

Orphanage to see young Will Wilder and, having formed the habit, he went on doing it year after year; became a kind of adopted uncle and, as there was nobody else to do it, took Will for trips to the zoo and the pantomime, days at the beach, and weekends canoeing on the river. No real relatives ever turned up to claim the boy. Nor did the doctor ever marry and have children of his own; somehow he was always too busy looking after his patients to have time for courtship; so a closeness grew between the two of them as year followed year.

Young Will never made friends at school. He was a silent, inturned boy, and kept himself to himself. For one thing his odd foot made him lame, so he could not run fast; he was no good at football or sports, which helped separate him from the others. But though he could not run he loved speed, and went for long rides on a bicycle the doctor gave him; also he loved books and would sit reading for hours on end while everyone else was running and fighting in the playground. And, from being a silent, solitary boy he became a thoughtful, solitary young man. He did well at his exams, but seemed to find it hard to decide on a career. While he was thinking, he took a job in the public library, and lived on his own in a bed-sitter. But he still called in on the doctor once or twice a week.

One time when he called in he said, "I've been reading up the old history of this neighborhood. And I found that way back, centuries back, there was a whole tribe of Wilders living in these parts."

"Is that so?" said the doctor with interest. "Maybe they were your ancestors. Maybe that was why your parents were traveling here, from Canada, to find the place their fore-fathers had come from. What did they do, those Wilders? Where did they live?"

"They were gypsies and tinkers and charcoal burners," Will said. "They lived in tents and carts on a piece of land known as Worplesdon Wilderness. I haven't been able to discover exactly where it was. It seems the Wilders had lived there so long — since Saxon times or before — that they had a sort of squatters' right to the land, although they never built houses on it."

"You ought to try and find an ancient map of the neighborhood," the doctor said, "and discover where it could have been." He glanced at his watch — not the watch he had buckled on a tree on the railway embankment, for somehow he had never found time to go back and reclaim that one, but another, given him by a grateful patient. Patients were always giving him presents, because he was a good doctor, and kind as well. "Dear me, how late it's getting. I must be off to the hospital; I promised to look in on old Mrs Jones."

They walked to the gate together, Will limping; then Will mounted the bike and pedaled swiftly away. "I wish something could be done about that foot of his," the doctor thought, sighing over the contrast between Will's slow, limping walk and his speedy skillful progress on the bike. During the years since Will's babyhood the doctor had read up all the cases of foot troubles he could find, from fallen arches to ingrowing toenails, but he had never come across any case exactly like Will's. "But there's that new bone specialist just come to the Wimbledon Hospital; I'll ask his opinion about it."

"I've found out a bit more about those Wilders," Will said, next time he called on the doctor. "They had a kind of a spooky reputation in the villages round about."

"Gypsies and people living rough often did in the old

days," said the doctor. "What were they supposed to do?"

"Anything from stealing chickens to hobnobbing with the devil! People were scared to go past Worplesdon Wilderness at night."

"I wish we knew where it had been exactly," said the doctor. "Maybe where the football fields are now. Oh, by the way, there's a new consultant, Dr. Moberley, at the Wimbledon Hospital, who'd very much like to have a look at your foot, if you'd agree to go along there sometime."

Will's face closed up, as it always did when his foot was mentioned.

"What's the good?" he said. "No one can do anything about it. Oh, very well — " as the doctor began to protest. "To please you I'll go. But it won't be any use."

"That certainly is a most unusual case," the consultant said to Dr. Talisman when they met at the hospital the following week. "The only thing at all similar that I've ever come across was a case in India, years ago."

"Could you do anything for him?"

"I'm not sure. I'll have to consider, and read up some old histories. I'll talk to you again about him."

But in the meantime Will came to the doctor one evening and said, "I've decided to go to Canada."

"Why go there?" Dr. Talisman was astonished. For, privately, he thought that in such an outdoor kind of place the boy with his lame foot would be at even more of a disadvantage. But Will surprised him still further by saying, "the museum has given me a small grant to do some research into legends about wolves."

"Wolves? I didn't know you were interested in wolves."

"Oh yes, I am," said Will. "I've been interested in wolves

for a long time. Ever since I was a child and you used to take me to the zoo, remember?"

Dr. Talisman did remember then that Will always stopped for a long time by the wolves' enclosure and seemed as if he would rather stay watching them than look at anything else in the zoo; as if he felt he could learn something important from them.

"You won't be going to Canada for good?" he said. "I shall miss you, Will."

"Oh no, I'll be back. I just want to go to a place where there are still wolves wild in the woods. And while I'm over there I'll see if I can find out anything about my parents. Do you remember, among my father's things there was a little book with a couple of addresses in a town called Wilderness, Manitoba? A Mrs Smith and a man called Barney Davies. Of course they may be dead by now but I shall go there and see."

"When are you off?"

"Tomorrow."

"But what about Dr. Moberley? He was going to think about your case."

"He wouldn't have been able to do anything," said Will, and limped down the garden to where his bike leaned against the fence.

"What about the Worplesdon Wilders? Did you find out any more about them?"

Will paused, his foot on the pedal.

"Yes," he said, "there was a tale in the Middle Ages that some of them practiced something called lycanthropy."

"Lycanthropy? But that's — "

"And there was one who lived in Saxon times — he was known as Wandering Will. He was supposed to come back every twenty years to see how his descendants were getting on. And when he came back — "

"Oh dear, there's my phone," said the doctor. "Just a minute. Don't go yet, Will."

But when the doctor returned from answering the phone, Will had cycled away.

"I wonder if he'll take his bike to Canada?" the doctor thought, looking after him.

✦   ✦   ✦

Will did; the great plains of northern Canada are wide and flat, endless pine forest and corn prairie, corn prairie and pine forest, through which the roads, straight as knives, run on seemingly for ever; wonderful roads they are for cycling, though you seldom see a cyclist on them. People stared in amazement to see the little dot that was Will come pedaling over the horizon, on and on across that huge flatness, sometimes under the broiling sun, sometimes in a fierce wind that had swept straight down from the North Pole.

Will was so quiet and serious, so straightforward and eager after knowledge, that people everywhere were ready to answer his questions. Yes, there were still wolves in the woods; yes, the Indians still believed that if you trod on a wolf's footprint you were drawn after him and must follow him helplessly day and night through the forest. And there were wolves in the prairie too, the Indians thought; when a wave of wind passed over those great inland seas of maize or wheat they would say, "Look, a wolf is running through the corn!" and they believed that when the last sheaf was harvested, the wolf who was hiding in it must be caught, or there would be no grain harvest next year.

Did the wolves ever attack people? Will asked. Opinions were divided on that; some said yes, wolves would follow a sleigh all day, and pounce on the travelers when dark came; others said no, wolves seldom or never harmed a man but preyed only on small game, rabbits, chipmunks, or wood-mice.

So Will went on, and at last he came to the town of Wilderness, which stood beyond the forest, on the edge of a great frozen swamp. Its wooden frame houses were so old, so grey, that they looked more like piles of lichen than human dwellings; not many people lived here now, and all the ones who did were old; they sat on their weathered porches in the sun all summer long, and in rocking-chairs by large log fires through the winter.

Will asked if Mrs Smith lived here still. No, somebody said, she died last winter. But yes, old Barney Davies was still alive; he lived in the last house on the left, before the forest began.

So Will went to call on old Barney Davies; a little shrunken wisp of a man, as weathered and grey as his house. He sat by a pine-knot fire, over which Will heated a can of beans that he took from his pack.

"Yes," said old Barney, eating his share of the beans, "your grandfather used to live here. A quiet fellow he was, come from farther east. And his son, your father, yes, he lived here too, married Mary Smith and they went off saying they'd be back. But they never came back. Your grandfather died a couple of years after they left. Friend of mine, he was. I've a few of his things still, if you'd like to see them."

"I'd like to very much," said Will, making coffee in an old kerosene tin. So Barney Davies rummaged in a wooden chest and presently brought out a rope of Indian beads and a tobacco pouch and a mildewed leather belt and a small oil-skin bag which held a wad of old, yellowed linen folded so damp and flat that Will had trouble prising it apart.

"Did my grandfather come from England?" he asked, holding the wad near the fire to dry it.

"Never said. Maybe he did. Never let on. Used to talk about England some. Made a living mending folks' pots and pans. A rare clever hand he was at that."

"What else did he do?"

"Used to spend a lot of time in the woods. Whole days, weeks together he'd be away. Not hunting or trapping. Never brought anything back. Seemed as if he was searching for something he never found."

By now Will had got the linen a bit dried and, very slowly, with infinite care, he unfolded it.

"Kind of an old map?" said Barney Davies, taking the pipe from his mouth. "Nowhere round here, though, I reckon."

"No," Will said, "it's an English map."

Ye Wildernesse of Whorplesdene, said the aged script across the top of the mildewed sheet. A river ran across the middle, the River Wey. Pine forests were drawn in one cor-ner, ash forests in another. Camp, it said, between the pine forest and the ash. Norman Village, in another corner. Pitch kettles, charcoal fire. And, crossways, a path seemed to be marked. By straining his eyes, Will thought he could just make out the inscription along the path — which seemed, as far as he could judge, to follow the track now taken by the main line from Woking to Guildford: he read the name aloud."Wandering Will's Way."

"Wandering Will," said old Barney. "I mind your grand-father talking about him."

"What did he say?"

"The Indians believe in something called the Wendigo," old Davies said. "Half man, half wolf. Runs through the forest. When you hear him, you have to follow. Or if you tread on his footprint, or if he crosses your track. Wandering Will was the same sort of critter, I reckon, only back in England. When he takes hold of you, he gives you a kind of longing for places where folk have never been, for things nobody knows."

"Yes I see."

"Want to keep the map?"

"May I?"

"Sure. It's properly yours. Well," said old Barney, "guess it's time for me to have my nap. Nice meeting you. So long, young fellow. Be going back to England now, I reckon?"

"Quite soon," said Will. He put the map carefully in his pocket, mounted his bike, and rode away along the road that skirted between forest and swamp.

He reckoned that before nightfall he ought to be able to reach the next town, Moose Neck, forty miles farther on.

But he reckoned without the weather.

In mid afternoon a few flakes of snow began to fall, and by dusk they had increased to a blizzard. Will did not dare continue cycling, he could not see ahead; there was nothing to prevent his going straight into the swamp, or into the river that crossed it.

He dismounted, tightened the strings of his parka, wrapped his waterproof cape round him, and huddled under the shelter of a spruce tree. Colder and colder it grew, darker and darker. The wind wailed through the forest like a banshee, like a mourning dragon, like a pack of starved dinosaurs. But in spite of the wind's roar, Will found it hard to keep his eyes open.

"I mustn't go to sleep," he thought. "To sleep in this would be certain death. But I'm so tired — so tired. . . I shall have to go to sleep. . ."

His eyes closed. . .

It seemed to him that he was not alone. All about him he could feel the nearness of live creatures, feel movement and stirring and warm breath. It seemed to him that he opened his eyes and saw many pairs of green lights, shining luminous in the dark; he knew they were the eyes of wolves. He could feel fur, and the warmth of bodies pressed tight against him.

"Don't be afraid," their voices were telling him. "Don't be afraid, we are your friends."

"I'm not afraid," Will said truly. "But why are you my friends? Most men are afraid of you."

"We are your friends because you are part of our family. You are the boy with a wolf's foot."

"Yes, that is true," said Will in his dream.

"You do not belong here, though. You must go back to the place you came from; you will not get what you are seeking here."

"What am I seeking?" Will asked.

"You will know when you find it."

"Where shall I find it?"

"In your own place, where the wolves hunt no longer, save in dreams, or in memory, or in thought, or in fear. In your own corner of your own land, where your forefathers were friends to wolves, where your cradle lay across the wolf's path. You must go back. You must go back."

"Yes," said Will in his sleep. "I must go back."

He sank deeper into warmth and darkness.

When he next opened his eyes, a dazzling sun was rising over the swamp. No wolves were to be seen; but all round the spruce tree were the prints of paws like dogs' paws, only bigger; a tuft of gray fur had lodged under a flap of Will's Parka. He tucked it between the folds of his map of Worplesdon Wilderness.

Then, through the loose, soft new snow he bicycled on to Moose Neck.

+ + +

When Will returned to England, he caught the 18.06 stopping train from Waterloo to Guildford. He got out at Worplesdon, left the station, climbed over a fence, and limped back along beside the track until he came to a piece of waste land, dotted all over with clumps of bramble, and with piles of bricks and stacks of old timber.

Then he sat himself down on the embankment beside a clump of willow, and waited.

It was dark. The wind was rising.

Presently he felt a puff of cold air on his cheek, and heard a voice in his ear.

"Well, my child? Finding me took you long enough, and far enough! Now you have found me at last, what do you want?"

"I'm not certain," said Will. "When I was younger I always wanted one thing — to be able to run faster than a train. But now — I'm not sure. I seem to want so many different things."

"Well, think carefully! If you wanted it, I could take away your wolf's foot; I could help you run faster than a train. Do you want to try?"

It seemed to Will that the cold wind caught him by the

arms; he was running along the grassy embankment — fast, faster — black air and signal lights streamed past him, there was a black-and-gold ribbon ahead of him; he caught up and overtook the 22.50 from Waterloo and raced into Guildford ahead of it. Then the wind swung him and took him to where he had been before.

"That was wonderful!" Will gasped, grabbing the old willow to steady himself. "But I know now that it's not what I want. I want to learn, I want to find out hundreds of things. Can you help me do that?"

"Yes, I can help you! Goodbye then, my child. You won't see me again, but I shall be with you very often."

"Goodbye, great-grandfather," said Will.

+ + +

Dr. Talisman was sitting late in his study, writing up his notes on the day's cases, when he heard his bell ring. He went to the door.

"Will! So you're back from Canada! It's good to see you — come and have some coffee."

"It's good to be back." Will limped into the doctor's study.

"So — did you hear many legends about wolves?"

"Yes I did," said Will. "And some true tales too."

"And did you find the town where your father had lived?"

"Yes I found it."

"By the way," Dr. Talisman said, "Moberley thinks he can operate on that foot of yours and cure your lameness; make you the same as everybody else."

"That's kind of him," said Will, "but I've decided I don't want an operation. I'd rather keep my foot the way it is."

"Are you quite sure?" said the doctor, somewhat astonished. "Well — you know your own mind, I can see. And have you decided on a career?"

"Yes," Will said. "I'm going to be a doctor, like you — Oh, I think this is yours: I found it tonight."

And he handed the doctor a tarnished old watch that looked as if it had been buckled round the branch of a tree for twenty years.

Acknowledgements

The following stories in the collection first appeared in NOT WHAT YOU EXPECTED: *The Boy with a Wolf's Foot, A Harp of Fishbones*; SMOKE FROM CROMWELL'S TIME: *The Gift Pig, A Small Pinch of Weather, The Lilac in the Lake, The Rocking Donkey, The King Who Stood All Night, Cooks and Prophecies, John Sculpin and the Witches, The Wolves and the Mermaids*; THE FAITHLESS LOLLYBIRD: *The Rain Child, The Night the Stars Were Gone, Moonshine in the Mustard Pot, Cat's Cradle.*

A Note on the Type

Shadows & Moonshine has been set in Monotype Bulmer, a type first cut in 1790 by William Martin for William Bulmer & Company's Shakspeare [*sic*] Printing Office, which was established during the reign of George III for the purpose of producing a new edition of Shakespeare's works. The type was revived with great sucess by ATF in 1928 and was soon made available for machine composition on the Monotype. While Bulmer draws from the tradition of Caslon, it is, like Baskerville, a transitional face, graced with characteristics that point toward the types cut by Giambattista Bodoni some decades later in Italy. More condensed than Baskerville, Bulmer reveals a debt to the Didot types in its increased contrast and refined serifs. Though it has been said that English printing suffered a general decline in the decades following Bulmer's death in 1830, the types that bear his name retained their luster to such a degree that no less a critic than Daniel Berkeley Updike would write, "They were very splendid of their kind."

✦   ✦   ✦

Design by Carl W. Scarbrough
Layout and composition by Susan H. Sims

Eclipse Fever by Walter Abish
352 PAGES; *036-5; $15.95

The American Boy's Handy Book by Daniel Beard
448 PAGES; 449-0; $12.95

The American Girl's Handy Book by Lina & Adelia Beard
504 PAGES; 666-3; $12.95

The Book of Camp-Lore & Wood Craft by Daniel Beard
288 PAGES; *352-6; $12.95

Borstal Boy by Brendan Behan
384 PAGES; 415-6; $14.95

La Bonne Table by Ludwig Bemelmans
446 PAGES; 808-9; $17.95

The Best of Beston by Henry Beston
224 PAGES; *104-3; $16.95

The Decline and Fall of Practically Everybody
by Will Cuppy
256 PAGES; 514-4; $14.95

How to Attract the Wombat by Will Cuppy
176 PAGES; *156-6; $15.95

How to Tell Your Friends from the Apes by Will Cuppy
160 PAGES; *297-X; $15.95

The Geography of the Imagination by Guy Davenport
400 PAGES; *080-2; $18.95

South Wind Through the Kitchen by Elizabeth David
416 PAGES; *309-7; $18.95

Aubrey's Brief Lives by Oliver Lawson Dick (ed.)
560 PAGES; *063-2; $20.95

Last Comes the Egg by Bruce Duffy
368 PAGES; *124-8; $17.95

Fillets of Plaice by Gerard Durrell
192 PAGES; *354-4; $15.95

Searches and Seizures by Stanley Elkin
320 PAGES; 253-6; $10.95

The Kitchen Book & the Cook Book by Nicolas Freeling
352 PAGES; 862-5; $17.95

Fiction and the Figures of Life by William H. Gass
304 PAGES; 254-4; $13.95

**In the Heart of the Heart of the Country
& Other Stories** by William H. Gass
240 PAGES; 374-5; $13.95

On Being Blue by William H. Gass
96 PAGES; 237-4; $11.95

Bright Stars, Dark Trees, Clear Water
by Wayne Grady (ed.)
334 PAGES; *019-5; $16.95

In the Springtime of the Year by Susan Hill
192 PAGES; 852-6; $10.95

Strange Meeting by Susan Hill
192 PAGES; 830-5; $10.95

A Distant Trumpet by Paul Horgan
656 PAGES; 863-1; $18.95

A Dresser of Sycamore Trees by Garret Keizer
224 PAGES; *154-X; $15.95

Cider with Rosie by Laurie Lee
240 PAGES; *355-1; $15.95

The Old Man at the Railroad Crossing
by William Maxwell
192 PAGES; 676-0; $10.95

Over by the River by William Maxwell
256 PAGES; 541-1; $10.95

The Autobiography of Michel de Montaigne
408 PAGES; *098-5; $17.95

Images and Shadows by Iris Origo
288 PAGES; *103-5; $15.95

Merchant of Prato by Iris Origo
448 PAGES; 596-9; $18.95

War in Val d'Orcia by Iris Origo
256 PAGES; 752-X; $10.95

Giving Up the Gun by Noel Perrin
136 PAGES; 773-2; $10.95

Hamlet's Mill
by Giorgio de Santillana & Hertha von Dechend
512 PAGES; 215-3; $20.95

The Maine Reader by Charles & Samuella Shain (eds.)
576 PAGES; *078-0; $19.95

Fading Feast by Raymond Sokolov
320 PAGES; *037-3; $16.95

Selected Poems of Herman Melville
by Robert Penn Warren (ed.)
480 PAGES; *269-4; $18.95

The Philosopher's Diet by Richard Watson
128 PAGES; *084-5; $14.95

The Philosopher's Demise by Richard Watson
128 PAGES; *227-9; $15.95

Dialogues of Alfred North Whitehead
400 PAGES; *129-9; $17.95

NB: *The* ISBN *prefix for titles with an asterisk is 1-56792. The prefix for all others is 0-87923.*